Th

The Vendetta

Honoré de Balzac

Translated by Howard Curtis

ET REMOTISSIMA PROPE

Hesperus Classics

Hesperus Classics
Published by Hesperus Press Limited
4 Rickett Street, London SW6 1RU
www.hesperuspress.com

First published in French, 1830
First published by Hesperus Press Limited, 2008

Introduction and English language translation © Howard Curtis, 2008

Designed and typeset by Fraser Muggeridge studio
Printed in Jordan by Jordan National Press

ISBN: 978-1-84391-176-0

CONTENTS

INTRODUCTION

As with most of Balzac's works, *The Vendetta* bears a precise date: January 1830. At that time – after an abortive attempt at establishing himself as a playwright, a few years of producing what we would now call pulp novels under a pseudonym, and a couple of disastrous business ventures – Balzac was just getting into his stride as a writer. The previous year, 1829, he had had his first major literary success under his own name with the historical novel *Les Chouans*. He was still some years away from conceiving the idea of a vast panoramic survey of contemporary French society, to be called *La Comédie humaine* (*The Human Comedy*), in which all his works were to be included, but he was clearly already seeing individual works as part of a series. *The Vendetta* was first published in book form in April 1830 as part of a volume (the first of two) entitled *Scenes from Private Life*, a title which was itself later to be given to a sub-category of the *Comédie humaine*.

This first volume of *Scenes from Private Life* carries a preface in which Balzac clearly states his determination to abandon historical romance (*Les Chouans* had been influenced by Sir Walter Scott) in favour of a new realism reflecting contemporary or near-contemporary society as rigorously as possible. At a time when romanticism was still the order of the day, he writes in this preface: 'all he [the author] is doing is giving back to the world what the world has given him.' *The Vendetta* needs to be seen, therefore, as one of Balzac's first attempts to introduce a new style of literature and establish himself as the realistic chronicler of his age.

Not that everything in the story was taken from life. Balzac was nothing if not a commercial writer: saddled with debts as he was, he knew he had to please the public and keep abreast of literary fashions. For *The Vendetta*, he almost certainly drew some inspiration from two recently published stories: Stendhal's 'Vanina Vanini', in which an aristocratic young Italian woman falls in love with a revolutionary whom she discovers hiding in her father's house, and Mérimée's 'Mateo Falcone', a violent tale set in Corsica, in which a father kills his own son in order to preserve his family's honour. Nor could *The Vendetta*'s story of lovers thwarted by a family feud fail to recall Shakespeare's *Romeo and Juliet* – indeed, Balzac himself makes reference to it in his text. *Romeo and Juliet* was a popular play in France at the time: three different translations of it were produced in 1827 and 1828. In addition, an Italian short story based on the play had recently appeared in a French translation, and Balzac almost certainly knew of it, as the publisher was a friend of his – so it is perhaps not mere coincidence, given that one of *The Vendetta*'s main characters is named Luigi Porta, that the writer of the Italian story was a man by the name of Luigi da Porto!

Nevertheless, true to Balzac's new realist credo, the main inspiration for *The Vendetta* was real life. Indeed, there is an intricate web of allusions to real characters and events in the story, a web which may be worth untangling as an indication, both of how closely Balzac hewed to reality and of how thoroughly he transmuted it into fiction.

The most striking character in the story, Bartolomeo di Piombo, the stern Corsican patriarch and follower of Napoleon, has a very specific real-life model: André Campi, who had been the lover of Balzac's first mistress, Antoinette de Berny, and the father of her illegitimate daughter Julie. Born in Corsica in 1765, Campi was a friend of the Bonapartes from his childhood days. He was particularly close to Napoleon's brother Lucien, and when Lucien was appointed Minister of the Interior, Campi became his secretary. He was also a confidant of the Bonapartes' mother, Laetitia, and lived for a time in her house. The Bonapartes often sent him on important missions abroad, usually in relation to their financial dealings.

André Campi and Antoinette de Berny were lovers for fifteen years, from 1800 to 1815. Although Campi died in 1819, and Antoinette and Balzac did not begin their liaison until a few years later, there is evidence that Balzac felt a degree of jealousy towards Campi: some years after the composition of *The Vendetta*, he referred to him as 'that terrible Corsican who took the youth' of Antoinette de Berny. This feeling is almost certainly reflected in the negative aspects of the character of Bartolomeo di Piombo as depicted by Balzac. (There may be a reference to Campi's fifteen-year relationship with Antoinette in Ginevra di Piombo's assertion to her father: 'For fifteen years I have not moved from beneath your protecting wing...' And of course, the dates – 1800–1815 – correspond exactly to those in the story.)

At the same time, Balzac takes care to emphasise Bartolomeo di Piombo's honesty, loyalty and dislike of pomp, all of which seem to have been characteristics of André Campi. Balzac would have had ample opportunity to hear about these various aspects of Campi's character, not only from Antoinette de Berny, but from the woman who took her place as Balzac's mistress, Laure d'Abrantès. Laure had been intimately acquainted with Napoleon's court through her late husband, who had been one of his generals. At the very period when Balzac was writing *The Vendetta*, he was also helping Laure to compile her multi-volume *Memoirs of the Empire*, in which André Campi naturally figures. In addition to the Campi connections, a number of other anecdotes Balzac would have heard from Laure also find their echoes in *The Vendetta*. For instance,

Laure's mother had once hidden a Corsican fugitive, whom Laure discovered by chance in their house, and the scene at the beginning of the story when an impoverished Bartolomeo encounters the Bonaparte brothers and asks for their help reflects an episode which Laure included in her *Memoirs*, involving yet another Corsican.

But it is the story of Ginevra's marriage and repudiation by her father which has the closest antecedents in real events – 'closest' in the sense of most personal, since these events were part of Balzac's own family history. The character of Ginevra may be partly based on Balzac's sister Laurence, who had died in 1825, some years after contracting a disastrous marriage which was heartily disapproved of by her parents. But even closer parallels exist with the story of Théodore Lassalle and Adolphe Midy. Théodore Lassalle was the half-sister of Eugène Serville, the husband of Balzac's other sister, Laure. Both Théodore and Eugène were illegitimate. When Théodore met and fell in love with Adolphe Midy, Adolphe's mother bitterly opposed their union, not only because of her proposed daughter-in-law's illegitimacy, but because there was a long-standing feud between their two families. Prevented from marrying, the couple had three children out of wedlock. Finally, when Adolphe reached the age of twenty-five, he was able to make a legal declaration (*acte respectueux* in French) – the same kind of declaration which Ginevra makes in *The Vendetta* – which allowed him to marry without parental consent. (In real life, Ginevra would have been able to make such a declaration at the age of twenty-one, as in French law at the time that was the age at which a woman was able to make an *acte respectueux*, compared with twenty-five for a man – but as if to emphasise the parallels, Balzac makes Ginevra twenty-five in his story, the same age at which Adolphe made *his* declaration.) Not that the legitimisation of their union made things easier for Adolphe and Théodore, given that Adolphe's mother had cut them off financially and refused ever to speak to them. Adolphe, who was a painter (a pupil of Jean-Baptiste Regnault, a well-known artist and teacher and the probable model for Servin in *The Vendetta*), was forced to make copies in order to earn a living, while his wife worked as a colourist. But they were barely able to make ends meet, and they died in poverty.

Knowledge of this real-life background may make it easier for the modern reader to accept what might seem like conventional or melodramatic elements somewhat at odds with Balzac's avowed realistic intentions. At first sight, the three protagonists appear to be stock characters – the stern, autocratic father, the dashing young officer, the beautiful, plucky heroine – and the final scenes do indeed descend into melodrama and almost seem to cry out for operatic treatment. (The penultimate scene, with the heroine dying in a garret while the love of her life looks on aghast and well-wishers crowd into the room, powerless to help, is oddly reminiscent of the end of Puccini's *La Bohème* – itself based on a French novel published less than twenty years after *The Vendetta*.) But not only is the story full of references to real situations, as we have seen, Balzac is also too acute an observer of human personality to present us with merely black-and-white characters.

Bartolomeo is indeed, on one level, a familiar figure: the harsh patriarch who thwarts his children's wishes. But Balzac goes to great lengths to introduce light and shade into this portrayal. From his model, André Campi, are derived Bartolomeo's probity and loyalty as a politician, but on a personal level he is also shown as an indulgent father with an almost obsessive love for his daughter. His defects are a mirror image of his virtues: the very same devotion and steadfastness that have made him so admirable in his political life are what make him so protective of his family's honour that he will refuse to abandon an old vendetta even if it costs him his daughter's love.

Ginevra is an equally nuanced portrait: not just a sweet young heroine, beautiful, intelligent and talented – a 'truly poetic creature', as Balzac calls her at one point – but also passionate and headstrong, and as stubborn as her father. In the Ginevra-Luigi couple, it is she who is clearly the stronger. Balzac makes much of the difference in their ages: although Luigi is highly experienced in warfare, he is barely out of his adolescence and is even referred to at one point as a child. Of the two, Luigi is the romantic dreamer, while Ginevra is the tough realist. It is Ginevra who takes a stand against her father and determines to press ahead with the marriage whatever the consequences, it is she who responds to Luigi's statement that only he has the right to work for the two of them with the assertion that they must 'share everything, pleasures and pains', and by the end it is she who is almost single-handedly keeping the household together, while Luigi is reduced to walking the streets of Paris, desperately seeking for a solution.

Balzac does not seem very interested in developing the character of Luigi, who remains the weakest of the three protagonists. The author's attention is reserved for Bartolomeo and Ginevra, two powerful, determined characters, neither willing to budge and both giving as good as they get, and it is the clash between these two which makes the story memorable. In the vast range of Balzac's novels and stories, *The Vendetta* may be a relatively minor work, an early attempt to demonstrate the validity of his new, realistic approach.

But, nourished by its real-life allusions, and anchored in two unforgettable characters, it is a fascinating harbinger of the glories to come.

– Howard Curtis, 2008

The Vendetta

To Puttinati
Milanese Sculptor

Towards the end of October 1800, a stranger, accompanied by a woman and a little girl, appeared outside the Tuileries in Paris, and stood for a long time beside the remains of a recently demolished house, on the spot where today there rises the unfinished wing intended to join Catherine de' Medici's chateau to the Louvre of the Valois. There he stood, arms folded, head tilted, raising his eyes only occasionally to look in turn at the First Consul's palace and at his wife seated beside him on a stone. Although the woman's one concern seemed to be the little girl, aged nine or ten, with whose long black hair she was playing, she was fully aware of her companion's glances. It was not so much love as another feeling which united these two creatures and imbued their movements and thoughts with the same anxiety. Poverty may well be the strongest of bonds. The stranger had a broad, solemn face, the kind of face so often painted by the Carraccis,[1] and thick black hair with a large admixture of white. Although his features were noble and proud, there was something harsh about them which detracted from these qualities. Strong as he still looked, and upright as was his posture, he was clearly more than sixty years of age. The worn state of his clothes announced that he had come from a foreign country. Although the woman's once beautiful, now withered face betrayed a profound sadness, whenever her husband looked at her she made an effort to smile and appear calm and composed. The little girl remained standing, even though her suntanned young face was marked with exhaustion. She had an Italian bearing, large black eyes beneath well-arched eyebrows, a native nobility and a true grace. More than one passer-by felt moved at the mere sight of this group, the members of which made no effort to conceal a despair as profound as its expression was simple. But that fleeting wellspring of kindness which distinguishes

3

the people of Paris quickly ran dry. No sooner did the stranger believe himself the object of some idler's attention than he would look at him with such a hostile air that even the most intrepid loiterer would hurry on his way as if he had stepped on a snake. Having stood there undecided for a long time, all at once the tall stranger moved his hand over his brow, as if to dismiss the thoughts which had furrowed deep lines in it, and made what must have been a desperate decision. After casting a sharp look at his wife and daughter, he took a long dagger from his jacket, handed it to his companion, and said in Italian, 'I'm going to see if the Bonapartes remember us.'[2] And he walked off, with a slow but confident step, towards the entrance of the palace, where he was naturally stopped by a soldier of the consular guard with whom he was unable to engage in long discussion. Taking note of the stranger's obstinacy, the sentry raised his bayonet by way of ultimatum. As luck would have it, at that moment the sentry was relieved, and the corporal very obligingly pointed the stranger to the place where the captain in charge of the guard could be found.

'Please inform Bonaparte that Bartolomeo di Piombo would like to speak to him,' the Italian said to the captain.

The officer tried to explain to Bartolomeo that the First Consul could not be seen unless an audience had first been requested in writing, but the stranger was insistent that the officer go and inform Bonaparte. The captain objected that he had his instructions, and refused categorically to obey this strange supplicant's command. Bartolomeo scowled fearsomely at the captain, seeming to hold him responsible for whatever misfortunes this refusal might bring about, then fell silent, folded his arms tightly over his chest, and went and took up position beneath the portico which leads from the courtyard to the Tuileries gardens. People who want something strongly enough are almost always well served by chance. Just as Bartolomeo di Piombo was sitting down on one of the bollards beside the entrance to the Tuileries, a carriage arrived, and Lucien Bonaparte, who was then Minister of the Interior, got out.

'Luciano!' cried the stranger. 'How fortunate for me that you are here!'

These words, uttered in Corsican patois, stopped Lucien in his tracks just as he was about to disappear beneath the archway. He looked at his fellow countryman and recognised him. Bartolomeo then whispered something in his ear, and Lucien led him into the palace. Murat, Lannes and Rapp were with the First Consul in his study. As soon as Lucien entered, followed by this strange figure, the conversation ceased. Lucien took Napoleon by the hand and drew him to the window. After a brief exchange of words with his brother, the First Consul made a gesture with his hand. Murat and Lannes obeyed and left the room, but Rapp, hoping to stay, pretended not to have seen anything. He only withdrew, reluctantly, after a sharp command from Bonaparte. Even then, the First Consul could hear Rapp's footsteps in the adjacent drawing room, and he abruptly went out and found him standing close to the wall between the drawing room and the study.

'Do you still not understand?' said the First Consul. 'I need to be alone with my fellow countryman.'

'A Corsican,' replied Rapp. 'I am too suspicious of such people not to – '

The First Consul could not help smiling. He took his loyal officer lightly by the shoulders and pushed him out of the room.

'Well, now, my poor Bartolomeo,' the First Consul asked Piombo, 'what are you doing here?'

'I'm here to ask you for refuge and protection,' Bartolomeo replied in a brusque tone, 'if you are a true Corsican.'

'What misfortune can have driven you from your country? You were the richest man there, the most – '

'I killed the whole of the Porta family,' replied the Corsican in a deep voice, knitting his brows.

The First Consul took two steps back, as if surprised.

'Are you going to betray me?' cried Bartolomeo, throwing Bonaparte a sombre look. 'Don't you know that there are still four Piombos left in Corsica?'

Lucien took his compatriot's arm, and shook him. 'Have you come here to threaten the saviour of France?' he said sharply.

Bonaparte made a sign to Lucien, who fell silent. Then he looked at Piombo, and said, 'Why did you kill the Portas?'

'We were friends again,' he replied. 'The Barbantis had reconciled us. The day after we drank to the end of our feud, I left them in order to attend to some business in Bastia. They remained in my house, and set fire to my vineyard at Longone. They killed my son Gregorio. My daughter Ginevra and my wife escaped: they had taken communion that morning, the Virgin protected them. I returned to find my house destroyed. As I walked through its ashes, my foot suddenly struck the body of Gregorio, whom I recognised by the light of the moon. "The Portas did this!" I said to myself. I immediately took to the *maquis*,[3] gathered together a few men to whom I had rendered services – do you understand me, Bonaparte? – and we marched on the Portas' vineyard. We arrived at five in the morning, and by seven they had all gone to meet their maker. Giacomo claims that Elisa Vanni saved a child, little Luigi – although I had tied him to his bed myself before setting fire to the house. I left the island with my wife, without having been able to ascertain if it was true that Luigi Porta was still alive.'

Bonaparte was looking at Bartolomeo with an expression of curiosity, but no surprise.

'How many of them were there?' Lucien asked.

'Seven,' replied Piombo. 'They were your persecutors in the old days.' These words did not rouse the two brothers to any expression of hatred. 'Ah, you are no longer Corsicans!' cried Bartolomeo, in a kind of despair. 'Farewell, then. I once protected you,' he added, reproachfully. 'Without me, your mother would never have reached Marseille,' he said, addressing Bonaparte, who stood lost in thought, his elbow propped on the mantelpiece.

'In all conscience, Piombo,' replied Napoleon, 'I cannot take you under my wing. I have become the leader of a great nation, I command the republic, and must make sure that its laws are obeyed.'

'Ah!' said Bartolomeo.

'But I can turn a blind eye,' Bonaparte went on. 'As long as the custom of vendetta persists, there can be no rule of law in Corsica,' he added, as if to himself. 'We must do everything we can to destroy it.'

Bonaparte remained silent for a moment, and Lucien made a sign to Piombo to say nothing. The Corsican was already shaking his head from side to side with a disapproving air.

'Remain here,' the First Consul continued, addressing Bartolomeo, 'and we will ignore it. First, I will make sure your properties are sold, so that you have the means to live. Then, in a little while, we will remember you. But forget your vendetta! There is no *maquis* here. If you use your dagger, you can expect no mercy. Here the law protects all citizens, and no one takes the law into his own hands.'

'He's made himself the leader of a strange country,' Bartolomeo replied, taking Lucien's hand and shaking it. 'But you have recognised me in my hour of need, and that makes us friends for life. You will always be able to rely on the Piombos.'

At these words, the furrows went from his brow, and he looked about him with satisfaction.

'You're well set up here,' he said with a smile, as if he wanted to live there himself. 'And you're dressed all in red like a cardinal.'

'Now it's up to you to succeed and have a palace in Paris,' said Bonaparte, looking his fellow countryman up and down. 'I may often need to have a loyal friend beside me in whom I can confide.'

A sigh of joy emerged from Piombo's vast chest. He held out his hand to the First Consul and said, 'You are still a Corsican!'

Bonaparte smiled. He looked silently at this man, through whom he was somehow breathing the air of his homeland, that island where once he had been saved so miraculously from the hatred of the English faction, and which he was never to see again. He made a sign to his brother, who led Bartolomeo di Piombo out. Lucien inquired with interest about the financial situation of their family's former protector. Piombo drew the Minister of the Interior to a window, and pointed to his wife and Ginevra, both sitting on a pile of stones.

'We came here on foot all the way from Fontainebleau,' he said, 'and we don't have a thing.'

Lucien took his purse and gave it to his compatriot. He advised him to come back the following day, when they would discuss ways to ensure the future well-being of his family. The value of all the property Piombo possessed in Corsica would barely suffice to let him live decently in Paris.

Fifteen years passed between the arrival of the Piombo family in Paris and the following adventure, which, without an account of these events, would have been less intelligible.

Servin, one of our most distinguished artists, was the first person to conceive the idea of opening a studio for young ladies wishing to receive painting lessons. Aged about forty, morally upright and entirely devoted to his art, he had married, for love, the daughter of an impoverished general. At first, mothers would bring their daughters to the studio themselves. Then, having become acquainted with Servin's principles and appreciated the care he put into deserving their trust, they allowed them to go alone. It was part of the painter's plan to accept as pupils only young ladies belonging to rich or respected families, so that no one could reproach him on the composition of his studio. He even refused to take young ladies who had a genuine desire to become artists, to whom he would have had to teach certain things without which no talent is possible in painting. Gradually, his prudence, the superior manner in which he initiated his pupils into the secrets of art, the mothers' certain knowledge that their daughters were in the company of other well-brought-up young ladies, and the sense of security instilled by the artist's character, morals and married state earned him an excellent reputation in the drawing rooms. Whenever a young girl expressed the desire to learn to paint or draw, and her mother sought advice, the answer was invariably 'Send her to Servin!' Servin thus became the specialist in painting for girls, just as Herbault was the specialist in hats, Leroy in fashions and Chevet in fine foods. It was acknowledged that, after taking lessons with Servin, a young lady could pass judgement on the paintings in the Museum, produce an excellent portrait, copy a canvas, and paint a genre scene. In this way, the artist met

9

all the needs of the aristocracy. Despite the relations he had with the best houses in Paris, he was independent, a patriot, and retained with everyone that light, witty, sometimes ironic tone, that freedom of judgement, which distinguishes painters. He had been scrupulous even in the layout of the premises where his pupils studied. The door leading from the street to the attic room above his apartments had been walled up. The only way to reach this retreat, as sacrosanct as a harem, was to climb a staircase from inside his home itself. The studio, which occupied the whole attic of the house, offered those vast proportions which always surprise inquisitive people who, having climbed sixty feet from the ground, expect to see artists living in a garret. It was a kind of gallery, abundantly lit by huge windows fitted with those large green serge curtains by means of which painters make use of the light. A host of caricatured heads, done as line drawings, in colour or with the point of a knife, hung on the dark grey wells, proving that, however great the difference in expression, the most distinguished young ladies have as much folly in their minds as men may have. A little stove and its great pipes, which described a terrifying zigzag before reaching the upper regions of the roof, were the infallible ornament of this studio. A shelf ran around the walls, and on it plaster casts lay in confusion, most of them covered in a pale dust. Here and there, below this shelf, the head of a Niobe hung in grief from a nail, a Venus smiled, a hand suddenly reached out like that of a poor man asking for alms; there were also a few smoke-yellowed *écorchés* looking like limbs torn the previous day from coffins, as well as paintings, drawings, dummies, frames without canvases and canvases without frames, which put the finishing touches towards giving this irregular room the appearance of a studio, distinguished by a strange mixture of ornamentation and bareness, poverty and wealth, care and neglect. Such an immense vessel, in which everything, even man, appears small, is like the backstage area of an opera house, filled with old clothes, gilded armour, scraps of material, and machines, but also with something as indefinably great as thought: genius and death are there; a Diana or an Apollo side by side with a skull or a skeleton, beauty and disorder, poetry and reality, rich colours in the shadows – a whole drama, motionless and silent. What a symbol of an artist's mind!

At the moment this story begins, the studio was lit by bright July sunlight, two rays of which streamed across its depth in broad translucent strips of gold, with specks of dust glittering in them. A dozen easels raised their sharp points, like the masts of ships in a port. Several young girls enlivened the scene with the variety of their countenances, their attitudes, their dress. The strong shadows cast by the green curtains, raised or lowered according to the needs of each easel, produced a multitude of contrasts, of surprising chiaroscuro effects. This group was the most beautiful picture in the studio. A fair-haired, simply-dressed young girl was working some distance from her classmates, diligently but with an apparent certainty of disaster; no one was looking at her, nor talking to her: she was the prettiest, the humblest and the least well-to-do. Two main groups, separated from one another by a slight distance, indicated that there were two societies, two spirits, even in this studio where rank and fortune ought to have been forgotten. Some seated, some standing, these young ladies, surrounded by their paintboxes, playing with their brushes or preparing them, wielding their glittering palettes, painting, talking, laughing, singing, unselfconsciously revealing their characters, comprised a spectacle unknown to men. One girl was proud, haughty, capricious, with black hair, beautiful hands and flashing eyes; another was gay, carefree and smiling, with chestnut hair, delicate white hands, a French virgin, lighthearted, without ulterior motive, living in the moment; yet another was dreamy, melancholy, pale, her head drooping like a dying flower; while her neighbour was tall, with narrow, dark, moist eyes and a Muslim languor, speaking little, but daydreaming as she cast surreptitious glances at a head of Antinoüs.[4] In the midst of them, like the *jocoso*[5] of a Spanish play, full of wit and epigrammatic sallies, one girl had her eye on all of them, making them laugh, and constantly lifting her head to show a face that was too lively not to be pretty: it was she who commanded the first group of pupils, comprising the daughters of bankers, notaries and merchants – all of them rich, but forced to endure the imperceptible but distressing scorn poured on them by the other young ladies, who belonged to the aristocracy. The latter were ruled by the daughter of one of the king's bailiffs, a little creature as foolish as she was vain, proud that her father held an office at court; she always liked to make it appear as though she understood their teacher's observations immediately and was only working as a favour to him; she used a lorgnette, always came late, beautifully attired, and asked her classmates not to raise their voices. In this second group, there were delightful figures and distinguished faces; but there was little innocence in these girls' eyes. Although they were elegant in their bearing and graceful in their movements, their faces lacked candour, and it was easy to see that they belonged to a world where etiquette shapes character from an early age, where the constant pursuit of social pleasures kills feeling and develops selfishness. When this gathering was complete, among these young ladies there were childlike heads, virgins of ravishing purity, faces with slightly parted mouths revealing virgin teeth, and smiling virgin smiles. The studio then resembled not so much a seraglio as a group of angels sitting on a cloud in heaven.

By midday, Servin had not yet appeared. For some days now, he had been spending most of his time in another studio of his, where he was finishing a painting for the exhibition. Suddenly, Mademoiselle Amélie Thirion, the leader of the aristocratic faction, turned to her neighbour and had a long talk with her. A great silence descended on the patrician group. Surprised, the bourgeois faction also fell silent, and tried to guess the subject of such a conference. But the young ultras' secret was soon discovered. Amélie stood up, took hold of a nearby easel and moved it to a spot some distance from the noble group, beside a rough partition wall which separated the studio from a small dark room used for keeping broken casts, canvases rejected by the professor, and supplies of wood for the winter. Amélie's action elicited a murmur of surprise, which did not prevent her from completing this removal by quickly shifting the paintbox and the stool close to the easel, as well as a painting by Prudhon[6] which her absent classmate was in the process of copying. After this revolution, the Right Wing got down to work, but the Left Wing held forth at some length.

'What will Mademoiselle Piombo say?' a young girl asked Mademoiselle Mathilde Roguin, the mischievous oracle of this group.

'She's not the kind of girl who'll say anything,' she replied. 'But in fifty years' time she'll remember this insult as if she had received it the day before, and will take a cruel revenge for it. She's someone with whom I would not like to be at war.'

'The banishment to which those girls have sentenced her is all the more unjust,' said another girl, 'in that the day before yesterday Mademoiselle Ginevra was very sad. They say her father had just tendered his resignation. This will merely add to her unhappiness, even though she was very good to those girls during the Hundred Days.[7] Did she ever say a word that could have hurt them? On the contrary, she avoided talking politics. But our ultras seem to be acting rather out of jealousy than out of party loyalty.'

'I'd like to take Mademoiselle Piombo's easel, and put it next to mine,' said Mathilde Roguin. She stood, but then thought better of it and sat down again. 'With a character like Mademoiselle Ginevra's,' she said, 'there is no knowing how she would take our kindness. Let's just wait and see.'

'*Eccola*,'[8] said the girl with dark eyes, languidly.

Indeed, the footsteps of someone climbing the staircase were just then echoing through the room. The words 'Here she is!' passed from mouth to mouth, and the most profound silence fell over the studio.

To understand the significance of the act of ostracism performed by Amélie Thirion, it is necessary to add that this scene took place towards the end of July 1815. The second return of the Bourbons had perturbed many friendships which had withstood the first restoration. It was a time when there arose within families, almost all divided in their opinions, the kind of deplorable scene which tarnishes the history of all countries at times of civil or religious war. Children, young girls and old people all shared the government's royalist fervour. There was discord in every household, and the most intimate actions and conversations were tinged with the sombre colours of mistrust. Ginevra Piombo idolised Napoleon. How could she have hated him? The Emperor was her fellow countryman and her father's benefactor. Of Napoleon's followers, the Baron de Piombo had been one of those most responsible for his return from the island of Elba. Incapable of renouncing his political beliefs, indeed eager to admit them, old Baron de Piombo remained in Paris, surrounded by his enemies. It was all the easier to view Ginevra Piombo with suspicion in that she made no secret of the sorrow which the second restoration had caused her family. Perhaps the only tears she had shed in her life had been drawn from her by the simultaneous news of Bonaparte's captivity on the *Bellerophon*[9] and the arrest of Labédoyère.[10]

The young ladies who comprised the aristocratic group belonged to the most fanatical royalist families in Paris. It would be difficult to give an idea of the exacerbated feelings of that period and the horror inspired by the Bonapartists. However insignificant and petty Amélie Thirion's action might appear today, it was at the time a perfectly natural expression of hatred. Ginevra Piombo had been one of Servin's first pupils, and the place she occupied was one that the others had long wished to wrest from her. Gradually, the aristocratic group had surrounded her: to drive her from a place which in a way belonged to her was not only to insult her, but to cause her a kind of grief – for all artists have a favoured place for their work. But political animosity may not have been the main reason for the behaviour of the studio's little Right Wing. As Servin's best pupil, Ginevra Piombo was the object of intense jealousy: the master admired both the character and the talents of this favourite pupil, and constantly used her work as a point of comparison. Although no one could quite explain the influence this young girl exerted over everything around her, she enjoyed a prestige within this little world which was not dissimilar to that of Bonaparte among his soldiers. In the last few days, the studio's aristocracy had resolved that this queen should be deposed – but, none of the girls having so far dared to distance herself from the young Bonapartist,

Mademoiselle Thirion had struck a decisive blow, thus making her classmates complicit in her own hatred. Although Ginevra was genuinely liked by two or three of the Royalists, who almost all followed their parents' line as far as politics were concerned, they judged it best, with the tact peculiar to women, to remain neutral in this feud. When she arrived, therefore, Ginevra was met with a profound silence. Of all the young girls who had so far come to Servin's studio, she was the most beautiful, the tallest, the shapeliest. She walked with a nobility and a grace which commanded respect. Her intelligent face seemed to glow with that animation peculiar to the Corsicans, an animation which in no way rules out composure. Her long hair, her eyes, her dark lashes expressed passion. Although her mouth was a little weak at the corners, with lips that were slightly too thick, it expressed that kindness which only strong people aware of their own strength possess. By a singular whim of nature, the charm of her face was somewhat belied by a marble brow on which was written an almost savage pride, a reflection of the customs of Corsica. That was the one link between Ginevra and her native land: in all the rest of her person, the simplicity and abandon typical of Lombard beauties were so appealing that only by ignoring her could one cause her the slightest pain. She exercised such a strong attraction that her old father always made sure that she was accompanied to the studio. The only defect of this truly poetic creature came from the very power of such a well developed beauty: she seemed to be a woman. She had rejected the idea of marriage, out of love for her father and mother, feeling that she was indispensable to them in their old age. Her taste for painting had replaced the passions which normally stir women.

'You are quite silent today, ladies,' she said, after taking a few steps in the midst of her classmates. Then she approached the

16

young girl who was painting at a distance from the others. 'Good day, my dear Laure,' she said in a gentle, affectionate tone. 'That head is really good! The skin is a little too pink, but the whole thing is wonderfully drawn.'

Laure raised her head and looked at Ginevra tenderly, and their faces lit up in an expression of mutual affection. A slight smile played on Ginevra's lips as she walked slowly to her place, apparently lost in thought, looking nonchalantly at the drawings or paintings, saying hello to each of the young girls in the first group, without noticing the unusual curiosity aroused by her presence. She was like a queen in her court. She paid no attention to the profound silence that reigned among the patricians, and walked past their group without uttering a single word. So preoccupied was she that she sat down at her easel, opened her paintbox, took out her brushes, put on her brown sleeves, adjusted her apron, looked at her painting and examined her palette as if unaware of what she was doing. All heads in the bourgeois group had turned to her. If the young ladies of the Thirion camp were not as openly impatient as their classmates, their glances were no less directed at Ginevra.

'She hasn't noticed a thing,' said Mademoiselle Roguin.

At that moment Ginevra abandoned the meditative attitude with which she had been contemplating her canvas, and turned to look at the aristocratic group. A single glance was enough to show her the distance separating her from them, but she said nothing.

'She can't believe anyone wanted to insult her,' said Mathilde. 'She didn't turn pale, and she didn't turn red. How annoyed those girls will be if she likes her new place better than the old one! – You are out of line over there, mademoiselle,' she said out loud, addressing Ginevra.

Ginevra pretended not to have heard, or perhaps she really did not hear. She stood up abruptly, walked rather slowly along the partition wall separating the small dark room from the studio, and appeared to examine the window through which the daylight came, attaching such importance to it that she climbed on a chair to raise the green serge curtain which blocked out the light. Having reached this height, she came level with a small crack in the partition wall, the true target of her efforts, for the glance she cast through it can only be compared to that of a miser discovering the treasures of Aladdin. She quickly got down, went back to her place, adjusted the position of her canvas, pretended to be dissatisfied with the light, moved a table to the partition wall, placed a chair on it, climbed nimbly onto this scaffolding, and again looked through the crack. She merely glanced into the small room, into which the daylight filtered through an open skylight, and what she saw there made such a powerful impression on her that she gave a start.

'You're going to fall, Mademoiselle Ginevra!' cried Laure.

All the girls looked at Ginevra as she tottered. The fear that her classmates might come running to her gave her courage, and she regained her strength and her balance. Swaying slightly from side to side on her chair, she turned to Laure and said in a voice full of emotion, 'Nonsense, it's even firmer than a throne!' She made haste to take off the curtain, got down, pushed the table and chair a long way from the partition wall, returned to her easel and shifted it a few more times, as if searching for a patch of light that suited her. She was little concerned with her painting: her true aim was to get closer to the dark room. By now she was beside the door, as she had wished from the first, and she began to prepare her palette, in complete and utter silence. From here, she was soon able to hear more distinctly the slight noise which, the day before, had so greatly aroused her curiosity and sent her youthful imagination racing across the vast field of conjecture. She soon recognised the deep, regular breathing of the sleeping man she had just seen. Her curiosity had been satisfied beyond her wishes, but now she found herself burdened with a huge responsibility. Through the crack, she had glimpsed the imperial eagle and, on a dimly-lit trestle bed, the face of a Guards officer. It all came clear to her: Servin was hiding a fugitive. She was terrified now that one of her classmates might come and examine her painting, and hear either the breathing of this unfortunate man or some louder inhalation, such as the one which had reached her ear during the last lesson. She resolved to remain close to this door, trusting her own skill to foil whatever fate might bring.

'It's better I stay here,' she thought, 'to prevent an unfortunate accident, rather than leave the poor prisoner at the mercy of a careless blunder.' Such was the secret of the apparent indifference with which Ginevra had greeted the discovery that her easel had been moved. She had been inwardly delighted by this move, as she had been able to satisfy her curiosity in a perfectly natural way. In addition, she had been too greatly preoccupied at that moment to seek the reason for the move. Nothing is more mortifying for young girls, as for everyone, than to see a spiteful act, an insult or a witty remark fall short as a result of the scorn with which it is treated by its intended victim. It seems that our hatred for an enemy increases in proportion to the degree to which he rises above it. Ginevra's behaviour was an enigma to her classmates. Her friends and enemies alike were surprised: every possible quality was attributed to her, except forgiveness for insults. Although Ginevra had seldom been given the opportunity to display this defect in her character during her time at the studio, the examples she had been able to give of her vindictive tendencies and her determination had nevertheless left a deep impression on the minds of her fellow pupils. After much conjecture, Mademoiselle Roguin concluded that Ginevra's silence betokened a generosity of spirit that was beyond praise; and, inspired by her, her circle decided to humiliate the aristocratic group. They achieved their aim with a volley of sarcastic remarks which shattered the pride of the Right Wing. The arrival of Madame Servin put an end to this struggle for supremacy. With that keenness which always accompanies spite, Amélie had noted, analysed and interpreted the phenomenal preoccupation which prevented Ginevra from hearing the polite but unpleasant argument of which she was the object. The revenge taken by Mademoiselle Roguin and her companions on Mademoiselle Thirion and her group had the inevitable effect of making the young ultras seek out the reason for Ginevra di Piombo's silence. Thus the beautiful Italian girl became the centre of attention, and was spied upon by both her friends and her enemies. It is no easy task to hide even the smallest emotion, the slightest feeling, from fifteen idle and curious young ladies whose wit and malice ask for nothing better than secrets to uncover, intrigues to create or thwart, and who can give all too many different interpretations to a gesture, a glance, a word, not to discover its true meaning. Thus Ginevra di Piombo's secret was soon in great danger of being found out. At that moment the arrival of Madame Servin produced an interval in the drama being silently played out within these young hearts, the feelings, thoughts, and progress of which were expressed by almost allegorical phrases, by wicked glances, by gestures, and by silence itself, which is often more intelligible than words. No sooner had Madame

Servin entered the studio than her gaze fell on the door beside which Ginevra now stood. In the present circumstances, this glance was not a random one. Although none of the pupils noticed it at first, Mademoiselle Thirion was later to remember it and find an explanation for the suspicion, fear and mystery which had imparted something wild to Madame Servin's eyes at that moment.

'Ladies,' she said, 'Monsieur Servin is unable to come today.' Then she complimented each girl, receiving in return a host of those feminine caresses which are as much in the voice and in the look as in the gesture. She soon came to Ginevra, overcome by an anxiety she found it hard to conceal. Ginevra and the painter's wife nodded to one another in a friendly fashion, but neither said a word: one painted, the other watched her paint. The soldier's breathing could easily be heard, but Madame Servin appeared not to notice it, and her dissembling was so pronounced that Ginevra was tempted to accuse her of deliberately turning a deaf ear. Meanwhile, the stranger moved in his bed. Ginevra stared at Madame Servin, and the latter said, without the slightest alteration in her expression, 'Your copy is as fine as the original. I'd have great difficulty choosing between them.'

'Monsieur Servin has not let his wife in on the secret,' Ginevra thought, answering Madame Servin with a sweet smile of incredulity, then humming a *canzonetta* from her country to cover the noise the prisoner might be making.

It was so unusual to hear the studious young Italian sing that all the girls looked at her in surprise. Later, this circumstance served as proof for the not very kindly assumptions of their hatred. Madame Servin soon left, and the session came to an end without further incident. Ginevra waited for her classmates to leave, as if she intended to remain behind and continue working for some time; but she unwittingly betrayed her desire to be alone, for as the pupils got ready to leave, she looked at them with barely disguised impatience. Mademoiselle Thirion, who in a few hours had become a cruel enemy to one who surpassed her in everything, guessed instinctively that her rival's feigned diligence concealed a secret. She had been struck more than once by the attentive air with which Ginevra had seemed to be listening to a noise that no one could hear. The expression which she caught in Ginevra's eyes at the end of the lesson was like a shaft of light to her. She was the last of the pupils to leave. She went downstairs to see Madame Servin, with whom she chatted for a moment, then pretended to have forgotten her bag and walked back up to the studio, where she found Ginevra standing on a hastily assembled pile of objects, so absorbed in the contemplation of the unknown soldier that she did not hear the slight noise produced by her classmate's steps. It is true that, to borrow an expression from Walter Scott, Amélie was walking as if on eggshells. She quickly went back to the door of the studio and coughed. Ginevra started, turned her head, saw her enemy, blushed, hastened to detach the curtain to allay suspicion of her intentions, put away her paintbox, and stepped back down. When at last she left the studio, she carried away with her, engraved in her memory, the image of a man's head as graceful as that of Endymion, the masterpiece by Girodet[11] which she had copied a few days earlier.

'That such a young man should be a fugitive! Who can he be? Surely not Marshal Ney?'[12]

These words are the simplest expression of all the ideas which Ginevra spent the next two days trying to interpret.

The day after next, although she tried as best she could to be the first to arrive at the studio, she found that Mademoiselle

Thirion, who had come by carriage, was there before her. Ginevra and her enemy looked at each other for a long time, although they both made sure their expressions were as inscrutable as possible. Amélie had seen the stranger's handsome face but, fortunately and unfortunately at one and the same time, the eagles and the uniform had not been visible through the crack in the door, and all she could do was conjecture. All at once Servin arrived, much earlier than usual.

'Mademoiselle Ginevra,' he said, after glancing around the studio, 'what are you doing over there? The light is bad. Come closer to the other girls, and pull your curtain down a little.'

Then he sat down beside Laure, whose work merited his most indulgent comments.

'Well now!' he exclaimed. 'There's an excellently drawn head. You're going to be another Ginevra.'

The master moved from easel to easel, scolding, flattering and joking – his jokes, as usual, being more feared than his reprimands. Ginevra had not obeyed his instructions, and remained at her post with the firm intention of not moving from it. She took a sheet of paper and began to sketch the head of the poor recluse in sepia. A work conceived with passion always bears a particular character. The ability to show nature or thought in their true colours is what constitutes genius, but passion often takes its place. Thus, in the circumstances in which Ginevra found herself, the intuition which she owed to the impact of that memory, or perhaps necessity, that mother of great things, lent her an uncanny talent. The officer's head was flung on the paper amid an inner trembling which she attributed to fear, and in which a physiologist would have recognised the fever of inspiration. From time to time she cast a furtive glance at her classmates, so that she could hide the drawing quickly in case of any inquisitive move on their part.

Vigilant as she was, there came a moment when she did not notice her implacable enemy hiding behind a large portfolio and staring through her lorgnette at the mysterious drawing. Recognising the face of the fugitive, Mademoiselle Thirion raised her head abruptly, and Ginevra clutched the sheet of paper in her hand.

'Why have you remained there despite my advice, mademoiselle?' Servin asked Ginevra gravely.

The pupil quickly turned her easel in such a way that no one could see her drawing except her master, and replied in a voice full of emotion, 'Don't you find, like me, that this light is more favourable? Wouldn't it be better if I stayed here?'

Servin turned pale. As nothing escapes the keen eyes of hatred, Mademoiselle Thirion became, as it were, a third party in the emotions stirring the master and the pupil. 'You're right,' said Servin, then added with a forced laugh, 'But you'll soon know more about that than I.' There was a pause during which the teacher contemplated the portrait of the officer. 'This is a masterpiece worthy of Salvator Rosa!'[13] he cried with all the enthusiasm of an artist.

At this exclamation, all the girls rose, and Mademoiselle Thirion came running with the speed of a tiger leaping on its prey. At that moment the fugitive, wakened by the noise, stirred. Ginevra knocked over her stool, uttered some incoherent phrases and started laughing – but she had already folded the portrait and thrown it in her portfolio before her formidable enemy had been able to see it. The easel was surrounded, Servin detailed in a loud voice the beauties of the copy his favourite pupil was making at that moment, and everyone was deceived by this ruse, except for Amélie who, placing herself at the back of her classmates, tried to open the portfolio where she had seen Ginevra put the drawing.

Ginevra seized the portfolio and placed it before her without saying a word. The two girls looked at each other in silence.

'Come now, ladies, back to your places,' Servin said. 'If you want to be as good as Mademoiselle de Piombo, you mustn't always be talking of fashions or balls, and malingering as you do.'

When all the girls had returned to their easels, Servin sat down beside Ginevra.

'Wasn't it better for this mystery to be uncovered by me than by another?' said Ginevra in a low voice.

'Yes,' the painter replied. 'You are a patriot. But, even if you were not, it would still have been you in whom I would have confided.'

The master and the pupil understood each other, and Ginevra no longer feared to ask, 'Who is he?'

'A close friend of Labédoyère, and the man most responsible, apart from the unfortunate colonel, for bringing together the Seventh Infantry Regiment and the grenadiers from the island of Elba. He himself was a colonel in the Imperial Guard, and has just returned from Waterloo.'

'Why haven't you burned his uniform and his shako?' said Ginevra sharply. 'Why haven't you given him civilian clothes?'

'They're being brought to me tonight.'

'You should have closed our studio for a few days.'

'He'll be leaving soon.'

'Is he so eager to die?' Ginevra said. 'Let him stay here until things quieten down a little. Paris is still the only place in France where a man can safely be hidden. Is he a friend of yours?'

'No, the only thing that commended him to me was his misfortune. This is how he came to be here: my father-in-law, who had re-enlisted during the campaign, met the poor young man, and very cleverly saved him from the clutches of those who arrested Labédoyère. The madman was trying to protect him!'

'Is that what you call him?' cried Ginevra, looking at the painter in surprise.

Servin was silent for a moment, then resumed, 'My father-in-law is under surveillance and can't keep anyone in his house. He brought him here one night last week. I had hoped to conceal him from all eyes by putting him in this corner, the only place in the house where he can be safe.'

'If I can be of help to you, use me,' said Ginevra. 'I know Marshal Feltre.'[14]

'Well, we'll see,' the painter replied.

This conversation lasted too long not to be noticed by all the girls. Servin left Ginevra and examined each easel in turn, taking so much time over his instructions that he was still on the staircase when the hour struck at which his pupils usually left.

'You have forgotten your bag, Mademoiselle Thirion,' he cried, rushing after Amélie, who had stooped to spying to assuage her hatred.

Expressing surprise at her absentmindedness, Amélie came back for her bag, while taking Servin's concern for her as one more proof that there was a mystery here, and clearly a grave one. She had already done all that needed to be done, and could say, like the Abbé Vertot, *My siege is over*.[15] She walked noisily down the stairs and slammed the door which led to Servin's apartment, in order to make it seem as though she had gone. Then she softly walked back upstairs, and stood behind the door of the studio. When Servin and Ginevra thought they were alone, the painter knocked in a particular way at the door to the small room. It immediately turned on its rusty, squeaky hinges, and a tall, well-built young man appeared. His imperial uniform made Ginevra's heart pound. The officer had his arm in a sling, and the pallor of his complexion indicated that he had suffered a great deal. On seeing a strange woman, he gave a start. Amélie, who could see nothing, was afraid to stay any longer; but it was enough for her to have heard the door creak, and she left without a sound.

'Have no fear,' Servin said to the officer. 'Mademoiselle is the daughter of the Emperor's most loyal friend, the Baron de Piombo.'

Having seen her, the young soldier had no doubts about Ginevra's patriotism.

'Are you wounded?' she said.

'It's nothing, mademoiselle, it's already healing.'

At that moment, the shrill, piercing voices of the street vendors reached the studio: 'Here is the sentence of death…' All three shuddered. The soldier was the first to hear a name that made him turn pale.

'Labédoyère!' he said, collapsing on the stool.

They looked at each other in silence. Drops of sweat formed on the young man's pallid brow, and in a gesture of despair he grabbed tufts of his own hair and laid his elbow on the edge of Ginevra's easel.

'All the same,' he said, getting abruptly to his feet, 'Labédoyère and I knew what we were doing. We knew what fate had in store for us, whether we succeeded or failed. He's dying for his cause, and I'm in hiding…'

He rushed towards the door of the studio, but Ginevra, nimbler than he was, darted forward and barred his way. 'Are you going to restore the Emperor?' she said. 'Do you think you can put the giant back on his feet when he himself could not remain standing?'

'What is to become of me?' the fugitive said, addressing both the friends whom chance had sent him. 'I don't have a single relative in the world, Labédoyère was my protector and my friend, I am alone. Tomorrow I may be exiled or imprisoned, I have never had any fortune other than my soldier's pay, I squandered my last crown to come here and try to snatch Labédoyère from his fate and take him away. Death is the one solution for me. When you're determined to die, you should know how to sell your head to the executioner. I was thinking just now that the life of an honest man is worth the lives of two traitors, and that a well-placed blow with a dagger can grant immortality!'

This fit of despair alarmed Servin, as it did Ginevra, who understood the young man well. Admiringly, she gazed at that fine head and listened to that delightful voice whose gentleness was barely altered by his anger. She suddenly spoke up, spreading balm on all the poor young man's wounds.

'Monsieur, with regard to your financial distress, allow me to offer you my savings. My father is rich, I am his only child, he loves me, and I am quite sure that he will not reprimand me. Don't have any qualms about accepting: all we possess comes from the Emperor, we don't have a centime we do not owe to his munificence. Is it not a sign of gratitude to be of service to one of his loyal soldiers? So take this sum with as little fuss as I make in offering it to you. It's only money,' she added, contemptuously. 'Now, as for friends, you'll soon find them!' She lifted her head proudly, and her eyes shone with an uncommon sparkle. 'The head that will fall to a dozen rifles tomorrow will save yours,' she went on. 'Wait for this storm to pass, and you can re-enlist abroad if you have not been forgotten, or in the French army if you have been forgotten.'

There is always a kind of delicacy, something maternal, provident and complete, in a woman's consolation. But when these words of peace and hope are complemented by graceful gestures and the kind of eloquence which comes from the heart, and above all when the benefactress is beautiful, it is difficult for a young man to resist. The colonel breathed in love through all his senses. His white cheeks were tinged with pink, his eyes lost a little of the melancholy that tarnished them, and he said in a distinctive tone, 'You are an angel of goodness! But Labédoyère! Labédoyère!'

At this cry, all three looked at each other in silent understanding. It was as if they had been friends, not for twenty minutes, but for twenty years.

'My dear fellow,' said Servin, 'can you save him?'

'I can avenge him.'

Ginevra quivered. Although the stranger was handsome, it was not his appearance that had moved her: the sweet pity which women find in their hearts for those in misery through no sin of their own had stifled any other affection in Ginevra. But hearing a cry of vengeance, finding in this fugitive an Italian soul, devotion for Napoleon, and a nobility that was quite Corsican… It was all too much for her, and she now looked at the officer with a respectful emotion which stirred her heart in the strongest manner. It was the first time she had ever had such an intense feeling because of a man. As any other woman would have done, she looked for a harmony between the stranger's soul and the refined beauty of his features, the felicitous proportions of his figure, which she admired as an artist. Led on by chance from curiosity to pity, from pity to a strong interest, she moved at last from that interest to feelings so profound that she thought it dangerous to remain there a moment longer.

'Until tomorrow,' she said, giving the officer her sweetest smile as consolation.

Seeing that smile, which seemed to light up Ginevra's face like the dawn, the stranger forgot everything for a moment.

'Tomorrow,' he replied, sadly. 'Tomorrow, Labédoyère – '

Ginevra turned, put a finger to her lips, and looked at him as if saying, 'Calm yourself, and be careful.'

Then the young man cried, '*O Dio! che non vorrei vivere dopo averla veduta!* (Oh, God! would I not want to live after having seen her?)'

The unusual accent in which he uttered these words sent a quiver through Ginevra.

'Are you a Corsican?' she cried, coming back to him, her heart racing with joy.

'I was born in Corsica,' he replied. 'But I was taken to Genoa when I was very young, and as soon as I was old enough for military service I enlisted.'

The stranger's beauty, the uncanny attraction lent him by his commitment to the Emperor, his wound, his misfortune, the very danger he was in, everything disappeared in Ginevra's eyes, or rather, everything merged into a single delightful new feeling. This fugitive was a child of Corsica, he spoke its beloved language! For a moment, Ginevra stood motionless, rooted to the spot by a magical sensation. Before her eyes was a living picture painted in vivid colours by all human sentiments combined, as well as by chance: at Servin's invitation, the officer had sat down on a divan, the painter had taken his guest's arm from its sling, and was busy undoing the bandage in order to dress the wound. Ginevra shuddered at the sight of the long, wide sabre cut on the young man's forearm, and let out a moan. The stranger looked up at her and began to smile. There was something touching, something that went to the very soul, in the care with which Servin was removing the linen and feeling the bruised flesh; while the wounded man's face, although pale and sickly, expressed, at the sight of Ginevra, more pleasure than suffering. An artist such as she was could not help but admire this conflict of feelings, or the contrast between the white linen, the bare arm, and the officer's blue and red uniform. The studio was bathed in a gentle half-light; but at that moment, a last ray of sunlight came to rest on the spot where the fugitive sat, in such a way that everything – his noble white face, his black hair, his clothes – was flooded with light. Being superstitious, Ginevra took this simple effect as a good omen. The stranger was like a heavenly messenger speaking the language of her homeland and captivating her with memories of her childhood, while in her heart there arose a feeling as fresh and pure as that first innocent age. For a brief while, she remained pensive, as if lost in infinite thought; then, blushing to think that her preoccupation was too obvious, she cast a gentle, rapid glance at the fugitive, and fled, still seeing him in her mind's eye.

There was no lesson the following day. Ginevra came to the studio, and Servin, who had a sketch to finish, served as mentor to the two young people and allowed the prisoner to remain with his compatriot. As they talked, they frequently broke into Corsican. The poor soldier recounted his sufferings during the retreat from Moscow: he had been present, at the age of nineteen, at the crossing of the Berezina, the one survivor of his regiment after all his comrades – the only men who had ever taken an interest in this orphan – had perished. In vivid strokes, he painted the great disaster of Waterloo. His voice was like music to Ginevra's ears. Raised in the Corsican manner, Ginevra was in her way a child of nature, she knew nothing of lies, and gave herself unhesitatingly to her impressions, confessing them, or rather hinting at them, without the petty, calculating game of coquetry played by the young ladies of Paris. More than once that day, she stood there, with her palette in one hand and her brush in the other, and the brush not even touching the palette: her eyes fixed on the officer and her lips slightly parted, she would listen, holding herself ready to make a brushstroke which she never made. She was not surprised to find such gentleness in the young man's eyes, for she felt her own eyes soften despite her desire to keep them either stern or calm. At other times, she would paint with unusual care for hours on end, without looking up, because he was there, near her, watching her work. The first time he sat down and gazed at her in silence, she asked him in a voice full of emotion, after a long pause, 'Does it amuse you to see me paint?' That day, she learned that his name was Luigi. Before parting, they agreed that, on the days when there were lessons in the studio, if some important political event took place, Ginevra would inform him by singing certain Italian melodies in a low voice.

The next day, Mademoiselle Thirion surreptitiously informed all her classmates that Ginevra di Piombo had a lover: a young man who, while the lessons were in progress, stayed in the small dark room adjoining the studio.

'You who take her side,' she said to Mademoiselle Roguin, 'keep an eye on her, and you'll see how she spends her time.'

And so Ginevra was watched with devilish attention. They listened to her songs, scrutinised her glances. Even when she did not think that anyone was watching her, a dozen eyes were constantly on her. Thus forewarned, the girls were able to interpret correctly the changing emotions on Ginevra's bright face, her gestures, the unusual accent in which she sang, and the attentive air with which she listened to indistinct sounds which she alone could hear through the partition wall. After a week, only one of Servin's fifteen pupils, Laure, had resisted the desire to take a look at Louis through the crack in the partition wall and, out of an instinctive weakness, was still defending the beautiful Corsican. Mademoiselle Roguin tried to detain her on the staircase as they left, hoping to prove to her the intimacy between Ginevra and the handsome young man by catching them together, but Laure refused to stoop to spying when it was unjustified by curiosity, and thus became the object of general disapproval. Soon, the daughter of the king's bailiff decided that it was unfitting for her to attend the studio of a painter whose opinions had a tinge of patriotism or Bonapartism, which, at that time, were considered one and the same thing. From that point, therefore, she stayed away, and Servin politely refused to go to her house. If Amélie forgot Ginevra, the evil seed she had sown bore fruit. Gradually, by chance, through idle gossip or out of prudishness, all the other girls informed their mothers of the strange adventure which was taking place in the studio. One day Mathilde Roguin did not come, the next day it was another of the girls, and finally the three or four young ladies who had been the last to remain also stopped coming. For two or three days, Ginevra and her young friend Mademoiselle Laure were the only occupants of the deserted studio. Ginevra did not even notice that she had been abandoned, and did not seek to discover the reason for her classmates' absence. Having so recently devised the means to correspond secretly with Louis, the studio had become a delightful retreat for her, a little world in which she was alone, thinking only of the officer and the dangers threatening him. Although she genuinely admired those noble people who are determined not to betray their political beliefs, she would urge Louis to submit as soon as possible to the authority of the king, in order to keep him in France, but Louis refused to submit, for fear of having to leave his hiding place. If passions only come to birth and grow under the influence of extraordinary or fantastic events, never did so many circumstances conspire to form a common bond between two people. Ginevra's friendship for Louis and Louis' for her thus made more progress in a month than a worldly friendship makes in ten years in a drawing room. Is not adversity the touchstone of character? Ginevra had the chance to get to know Louis and appreciate his qualities, and they soon felt a mutual respect for one another. Older than Louis, Ginevra found it a sweet sensation to be courted by a young man who was already so adult, so tested by fate, and who combined the experience of a man with the charms of adolescence. For his part, Louis felt an indescribable pleasure in letting himself be protected apparently by a young woman of twenty-five. Was it not a proof of love? The union of gentleness and pride, strength and weakness in Ginevra was irresistible, and Louis was totally captivated by her. They soon loved one another so deeply that they felt no need either to deny it or to confess it.

One day, towards evening, Ginevra heard the agreed signal: Louis was striking the panelling with a pin, in such a way as not to produce any more noise than a spider spinning its web. This was his method of asking permission to emerge from his retreat. She glanced around the studio, did not notice young Laure, and replied to the signal; but on opening the door, Louis saw Laure, and quickly went back inside. Surprised, Ginevra looked round, and now also saw Laure. 'You're here very late, my dear,' she said, walking over to her easel. 'This head seems to me finished, though. All it needs is a glint of light at the top of this plait.'

'It would be very good of you,' said Laure, in a voice full of emotion, 'if you could correct this copy for me, then I would have something of yours to keep…'

'I'd like that,' replied Ginevra, sure that once she had done this she could easily dismiss her. 'I thought,' she went on, making a few light brushstrokes, 'that you had a long way to go to get home.'

'Oh, Ginevra, I am leaving for ever!' cried the girl, sadly.

Ginevra was not as affected by these melancholy words as she would have been a month earlier. 'Are you leaving Monsieur Servin?' she asked.

'Haven't you noticed, Ginevra, that we've been the only two people here for some time?'

'That's true,' replied Ginevra, as if struck by a sudden memory. 'Are these young ladies ill, are they getting married, or are their fathers all on duty at the palace?'

'They have all left Monsieur Servin,' replied Laure.

'Why?'

'Because of you, Ginevra.'

'Because of me!' echoed Ginevra, and rose to her feet, with a proud air, a menacing brow and sparkling eyes.

'Oh, don't be cross, my dear Ginevra!' cried Laure in a sorrowful voice. 'But my mother wants me to leave the studio too. All the girls said that you were having a love affair, that Monsieur Servin let a young man who's in love with you stay in the dark room. I never believed these calumnies and said nothing to my mother. Last night, Madame Roguin met my mother at a ball and asked her if she was still sending me here. When my mother replied in the affirmative, she repeated those girls' lies. Mother told me off, saying that I must have known all about it, that I had failed in the trust that exists between a mother and her daughter by not telling her. Oh, my dear

Ginevra! I took you as my model, and now I can no longer be your classmate…'

'We'll meet again in life,' said Ginevra. 'Girls marry…'

'When they are rich,' replied Laure.

'Come and see me, my father has money…'

'Ginevra,' Laure went on, tenderly, 'Madame Roguin and my mother are supposed to be coming tomorrow to see Monsieur Servin and reprimand him, unless he is forewarned.'

If a lightning bolt had fallen at Ginevra's feet, it would have been less of a surprise to her than this revelation. 'What business is it of theirs?' she said, innocently.

'Everyone thinks it's very bad. Mother says it's immoral…'

'And you, Laure, what do you think?'

Laure looked at Ginevra, and their minds were as one; unable any longer to hold back her tears, Laure threw her arms round her friend's neck and kissed her. At that moment, Servin arrived.

'Mademoiselle Ginevra,' he said, enthusiastically, 'I've finished my painting, it's being varnished. What's the matter? The girls all seem to be on holiday, or in the country.'

Laure dried her tears, said goodbye to Servin, and withdrew.

'The studio has been deserted for several days,' said Ginevra. 'They'll never come back.'

'Nonsense!'

'Don't laugh,' Ginevra went on. 'Listen to me: I am the unwitting cause of the loss of your reputation.'

'My reputation?' the artist said, with a smile. 'But my painting is to be exhibited in a few days.'

'This has nothing to do with your talent, it has to do with your morals. The girls have spread the word that Louis was hiding here, and that you agreed to… to our love…'

'There is some truth in that, mademoiselle,' Servin replied. 'Those girls' mothers are prudes. If they had come to see me, all would have been explained. But what do I care about such things? Life is too short!'

And the painter raised his hand above his head and clicked his fingers. Louis, who had heard part of this conversation, came running immediately.

'You're going to lose all your pupils,' he cried. 'I will have ruined you.'

The artist took Louis's hand and Ginevra's and joined them. 'Will you marry, my children?' he asked them with touching affability. They both lowered their eyes, and their silence was the first confession they had made to each other of their love. 'Well,' Servin went on, 'you will be happy, won't you? Is there anything that can buy the happiness of two creatures such as you?'

'I am rich,' said Ginevra, 'and you will allow me to compensate you…'

'Compensate me?' cried Servin. 'When it becomes known that I have fallen victim to the calumnies of a few silly girls, and that I was hiding a fugitive, why, all the liberals in Paris will send me their daughters! I'm the one who may be in your debt then…'

Louis shook his protector's hand, unable to utter a word. But at last he said in a voice full of tenderness, 'So it is to you that I will owe all my happiness.'

'Be happy, I unite you!' said the painter, placing his hands on the heads of the two lovers in comical benediction.

This artist's jest put an end to the emotional scene. The three of them looked at one another and laughed. Ginevra took Louis's hand and squeezed it hard, with a directness worthy of the customs of her land.

'Ah, my dear children,' Servin resumed, 'do you think everything will be perfect now? Well, you are mistaken.'

The two lovers looked at him in surprise.

'Don't worry, I am the only one who has been put in a difficult position by your games! But Madame Servin is a little strait-laced, and I really don't know how we're going to deal with her.'

'Oh, God!' Ginevra exclaimed. 'I almost forgot! Tomorrow, Madame Roguin and Laure's mother are meant to be coming here to see you and – '

'I understand!' the painter cut in.

'But you can justify yourself,' Ginevra went on, with a proud toss of her head. 'Monsieur Louis,' she said turning to look at him keenly, 'must surely have lost his antipathy towards the royalist government by now, mustn't he? – Well,' she went on, seeing him smile, 'tomorrow morning I shall send a petition to one of the most influential people at the Ministry of War, a man who could never refuse the daughter of the Baron de Piombo. We'll obtain a tacit pardon for Major Louis, as they won't want to recognise you as a colonel. And then,' she said, turning to Servin, 'you'll be able to confound the mothers of my kind classmates by telling them the truth.'

'You're an angel!' exclaimed Servin.

While this scene was taking place in the studio, Ginevra's father and mother were waiting impatiently for her to return.

'It's six o'clock,' cried Bartolomeo, 'and Ginevra is still not back.'

'She's never before come home so late,' replied his wife.

The two old people looked at each other with all the signs of unusual anxiety. Too agitated to remain where he was, Bartolomeo rose and twice did a complete circuit of his drawing room – quite nimbly for a man of seventy-seven. Thanks to his robust constitution, he had changed little since the day of his arrival in Paris and, despite his height, he still held himself erect. His hair had become white and sparse, revealing a broad, protuberant skull which gave an exalted idea of his character and steadfastness, and his face was more deeply lined than before, while retaining that pale colouring which inspires veneration. The heat of passion was still visible in the uncanny gleam of his eyes, as fearsomely mobile as ever, the brows not yet entirely white. It was a stern face, but it was clear that Bartolomeo was entitled to be thus. His kindness and gentleness were hardly known except to his wife and daughter. In his duties or in the company of strangers, he never abandoned the majesty which time had imprinted on his person, and his habit of knitting his thick brows and contracting his features, which gave his gaze a Napoleonic steadiness, made him a difficult man to approach. In the course of his political life, he had been so widely feared that he was thought of as not very sociable; but it is not difficult to explain the causes of this reputation. Piombo's life, manners and loyalty were a reproach to most courtiers. Despite the delicate missions with which he had been entrusted, and which would have been lucrative for anyone else, he had an income of no more than about thirty thousand livres from his inclusion in the Great Book. If we think of the cheapness of government bonds during the Empire and Napoleon's generosity towards those of his loyal servants who knew how to open their mouths, it is easy to see that the Baron de Piombo was a man of strict probity. He was only a baron because Napoleon had had to give him a title when sending him to foreign courts. Bartolomeo had always professed an implacable hatred for the traitors with whom Napoleon surrounded himself in the belief that he could win them over with his victories. It was he, it was said, who had walked to the door of the Emperor's study, after advising him to rid himself of three men in France, the day before he left for his famous, and brilliant, campaign of 1814. Since the second return of the Bourbons, Bartolomeo had stopped wearing his Légion d'honneur. There was no finer image of those old republicans, incorruptible friends of the Empire, who remained as the living relics of the two most energetic governments the world has ever known. Although the Baron de Piombo was disliked by some of the courtiers, he counted Daru,[16] Drouot[17] and Carnot[18] among his friends. As for the rest of the politicians, since Waterloo they had meant as little to him as the puffs of smoke from his cigar.

Bartolomeo di Piombo had acquired, for the fairly modest sum which the Emperor's mother had given him for his properties in Corsica, the former Portenduère mansion, but had made no changes in it. Having almost always been housed at the expense of the government, he had only been living in this house since the disaster of Fontainebleau.[19] As is common with simple, virtuous people, the baron and his wife cared nothing for outward pomp: all the furnishings had belonged to the previous owners. The large, dark, bare, high-ceilinged apartments of this house, the wide mirrors in their old, gilded, almost black frames, and the furniture dating from the time of Louis XIV were in keeping with Bartolomeo and his wife, characters worthy of antiquity. Under the Empire and during the Hundred Days, holding a well-paid post, the old Corsican had had a great household establishment, but rather with the aim of honouring his position than out of any desire to shine. His life and that of his wife were so frugal, so tranquil, that their modest fortune was sufficient for their needs. Their daughter Ginevra meant more to them than all the riches in the world. When, therefore, in May 1814, the Baron de Piombo had given up his position, dismissed his staff and closed the door of his stable, Ginevra, who was as simple and unpretentious as her parents, had had no regrets: like the noble soul that she was, she found luxury in the strength of her feelings, just as she sought happiness in solitude and work. Besides, these three people loved each other too much for outward appearance to have any value in their eyes. Often, and above all since the second, terrible fall of Napoleon, Bartolomeo and his wife would spend delightful evenings listening to Ginevra playing the piano or singing. They took a great and secret pleasure in their daughter's presence, in her slightest word, they would watch her with tender concern, they would listen for her steps in the courtyard, however light they might be. Like lovers, all three of them could spend hours on end without speaking, their souls more eloquent in silence than in words. This profound feeling, the very life of the two old people, underlay all their thoughts. Theirs were not three lives but only one, like a flame divided into three tongues of fire. If sometimes the memory of Napoleon's generosity and downfall, or the politics of the day, overcame the two old people's constant solicitude, they could speak about it without shattering the community of their thoughts, for did not Ginevra share their political passions? What could be more natural than the fervour with which they took refuge in the heart of their only child? Previously, the demands of public life had absorbed all the Baron de Piombo's energies; but in renouncing his post, he needed to channel them into the last sentiment that remained to him. Moreover, apart from the usual ties that bind a father and a mother to their daughter, there was perhaps, unknown to these three despotic souls, a powerful reason for the fanaticism of their mutual passion: their love for each other was absolute. Ginevra's heart belonged entirely to her father, just as his belonged to her. Lastly, if it is true that we are attached to one another more through our faults than through our qualities, Ginevra shared all her father's passions to a remarkable extent. That was the origin of the only imperfection in the lives of these three people: Ginevra was extremely strong-willed, and just as vindictive and quick-tempered as Bartolomeo had been in his youth. Piombo took delight in developing these savage feelings in his daughter's heart, in exactly the same way as a lion teaches his cubs to swoop on their prey. But as this apprenticeship in vengeance could in a way only be conducted within the family home, Ginevra never forgave her father anything, and he always had to yield to her. Piombo saw only childishness in these feigned feuds, but the child acquired through them the habit of dominating her parents. In the midst of these storms which Bartolomeo liked to arouse, a tender word or look was enough to calm their angry souls, and they were never so close to a kiss as when they were threatening one another. Nevertheless, for the past five years or so, Ginevra, who had become wiser than her father, had been continually avoiding this kind of scene. Her loyalty, her devotion, the love which prevailed in all her thoughts and her admirable common sense had seen off her rages; but a great ill had nevertheless resulted from all this: Ginevra lived with her father and mother on a footing of equality which could not help but be harmful. To complete this list of the changes which had befallen these three people since their arrival in Paris, Piombo and his wife, neither of them well educated, had let Ginevra study as the fancy took her. Following her girlish whims, she had learned everything and abandoned everything, picking up and dropping every idea in turn, until painting became her ruling passion; she would have been perfect, if her mother had been capable of directing her studies, of lighting the way for her and harmonising her natural gifts: her faults came from the harmful upbringing which the old Corsican had taken pleasure in giving her.

Having made the floorboards creak beneath his feet for a while, the old man rang a bell. A servant appeared.

'Go and meet Mademoiselle Ginevra,' he said.

'I've always regretted that we no longer have a carriage for her,' observed the baroness.

'She didn't want one,' Piombo replied, looking at the baroness, who, accustomed for forty years to playing the role of an obedient wife, lowered her eyes.

Already in her seventies, tall, thin, pale and wrinkled, the baroness bore a perfect likeness to the old women in Schnetz's Italian genre paintings.[20] Usually she was so silent that she might have been taken for a new Mrs Shandy; but a word, a look, a gesture were enough to reveal that her feelings had retained the vigour and freshness of youth. Her clothes, devoid of style, often lacked taste. Most of the time she sat passively, buried in a wing chair, like a Valide Sultan,[21] waiting for or admiring her Ginevra, her pride and her life. Her daughter's beauty, stylishness and charm seemed to have become hers. If Ginevra was happy, then everything was well with her. Her hair had turned white, and a few wisps were visible above her white, wrinkled brow, or framing her hollow cheeks.

'For the last two weeks or so,' she said, 'Ginevra has been coming home a little later than usual.'

'Jean won't be quick enough,' cried the old man impatiently. He folded the tails of his blue coat, picked up his hat, pulled it down onto his head, took his cane and left.

'You won't get far,' his wife called out to him.

In fact, the carriage entrance had opened and closed, and she could hear Ginevra's steps in the courtyard. Bartolomeo suddenly reappeared carrying his daughter in triumph, while she struggled in his arms.

'Here she is, *la Ginevra, la Ginevrettina, la Ginevrina, la Ginevrola, la Ginevretta, la Ginevra bella!*'

'Father, you're hurting me.'

He immediately put her down, with a kind of respect. She shook her head gracefully, as if to reassure her terrified mother and tell her it was only make-believe. Colour returned to the baroness' pale, lifeless face, as well as a kind of gaiety. Piombo rubbed his hands vigorously, the clearest symptom of his joy: he had picked up this habit at court, seeing Napoleon lose his temper with those of his generals or ministers who had served him badly or who had committed some fault. Once the muscles of his face relaxed, the slightest wrinkle on his brow expressed benevolence. At that moment, these two old people were just like ailing plants restored to life by a little water after a long drought.

'Let's eat!' exclaimed the baron, offering his broad hand to Ginevra and calling her Signora Piombellina, another symptom of his gaiety, to which his daughter replied with a smile.

'By the way,' said Piombo as he left the table, 'do you know what your mother said to me earlier? That in the past month you have been staying much longer than usual in that studio of yours. It seems as though painting has become more important than us.'

'Oh, father!'

'Ginevra must have some surprise in store for us,' said her mother.

'Are you going to bring us a painting of yours?' cried the baron, clapping his hands.

44

'Yes, I am very busy at the studio,' she replied.

'What is it, Ginevra?' her mother asked. 'You've turned pale!'

'No!' cried Ginevra, with a sudden resolute gesture. 'No, let it not be said that Ginevra Piombo was ever a liar.'

Hearing this singular exclamation, Piombo and his wife looked at their daughter in surprise.

'I'm in love with a young man,' she said, in a voice full of emotion.

Then, without daring to look at her parents, she lowered her wide lids, as if to conceal the fire in her eyes.

'Is he a prince?' her father asked, assuming an ironic tone which struck fear into both mother and daughter.

'No, father,' she replied, modestly, 'he is a young man with no fortune…'

'Is he handsome, then?'

'He is unhappy.'

'What does he do?'

'He's a comrade of Labédoyère's, a fugitive. Servin has been hiding him, and – '

'Servin is an honest fellow who acted well,' cried Piombo. 'But you have acted badly, daughter, loving a man other than your father…'

'I cannot choose not to love,' replied Ginevra, gently.

'I flattered myself,' her father went on, 'that my Ginevra would be faithful to me until I died, that the care and attention she received from her mother and myself would be enough for her, that our love for her would have no rival in her soul, and that – '

'Have I ever reproached you for your fanatical devotion to Napoleon?' said Ginevra. 'Have you loved only me? Haven't you been away on missions for months on end? Haven't

I borne your absences courageously? There are necessities in life to which we must submit.'

'Ginevra!'

'No, you don't love me for myself, and your reproaches betray an intolerable selfishness.'

'You are blaming your father's love,' cried Piombo, his eyes ablaze.

'Father, I will never blame you,' replied Ginevra, more gently than her mother, who was trembling with fear, had expected. 'You are justified in your selfishness, just as I am justified in my love. As heaven is my witness, never has a daughter more faithfully done her duty to her parents. I have never seen anything but happiness and love where others tend to see nothing but obligation. For fifteen years I have not moved from beneath your protecting wing, and it has been a sweet pleasure for me to enchant your days. But would I therefore be ungrateful in giving myself to the charm of loving, in desiring a husband to protect me after you?'

'Are you bargaining with your father now, Ginevra?' asked the old man in a gloomy tone.

There followed an alarming pause, during which nobody dared to speak. At last, Bartolomeo broke the silence, crying in a heartrending voice, 'Stay with us, stay with your old father! I couldn't bear to see you loving a man. Ginevra, you haven't long to wait to be free...'

'But, father, think of this. We will not leave you. The two of us will love you, and you will have a chance to get to know the man in whose care you will leave me! You will be doubly cherished, by me and by him – for he is me and I am totally him.'

'Oh, Ginevra! Ginevra!' cried the baron, clenching his fists. 'Why didn't you marry when Napoleon had accustomed me to the idea and was introducing you to dukes and counts?'

'They loved me to order,' said the girl. 'Besides, I didn't want to leave you, and they would have taken me away with them.'

'You do not want to leave us,' said Piombo. 'But if you marry, you will cut us off! I know you, my daughter, you will stop loving us.' He turned to his wife, who had not moved and sat there as if stunned. 'Elisa, we no longer have a daughter, she wants to marry.'

The old man raised his hands in the air as if to call upon God. Then he sat down, his body bent, as if weighed down with sorrow. Ginevra could see how agitated her father was, and the way he restrained his anger broke her heart. She had been expecting him to fly into a rage, and had not armed her soul against paternal gentleness.

'No, father,' she said, in a touching voice, 'you will never be abandoned by your Ginevra. But love her also a little for herself. If only you knew how much *he* loves me! Oh, it could never be he who would cause me pain!'

'You're already making comparisons,' cried Piombo, in a fearsome tone. 'No, I cannot bear the idea. If he loved you as you deserve to be loved, he would kill me, and if he did not love you, I would take my dagger to him.'

Piombo's hands were shaking, his lips were shaking, his whole body was shaking. His eyes blazed with anger; Ginevra alone could sustain his gaze, for at such times her eyes would light up, and the daughter would be fully worthy of the father.

'Love you?' he resumed. 'Who is the man worthy of such a life? To love you like a father, is that not already to live in paradise? Who therefore will ever be worthy of being your husband?'

'*He* will,' said Ginevra, 'although I feel unworthy of him.'

'He?' Piombo repeated mechanically. 'Who do you mean?'

'The man I love.'

'How can he possibly know you well enough to love you?'

'But, father,' Ginevra went on, with a touch of impatience, 'even if he didn't love me, as long as I love him – '

'So you love him, do you?' cried Piombo.

Ginevra gently bowed her head.

'Do you love him more than us?'

'These two feelings cannot be compared,' she replied.

'One is stronger than the other,' Piombo went on.

'I think so,' Ginevra said.

'You shan't marry him!' the baron cried, and his voice rattled the windows in the drawing room.

'I *will* marry him,' answered Ginevra, calmly.

'My God! my God!' her mother cried. 'Where will this quarrel end? *Santa Virginia*, intercede between them!'

The baron, who had been striding up and down, came and sat down. His face clouded over, became glacially stern, and he looked straight at his daughter and said to her in a weak, soft voice, 'No, Ginevra, you shan't marry him. Don't say you will, not this evening. Let me believe the contrary. Do you want to see your father on his knees, his white head bowed before you? I'm begging you…'

'Ginevra Piombo has not been brought up to make a promise and then not keep it,' she replied. 'I am your daughter.'

'She's right,' said the baroness. 'We are put on this earth to marry.'

'So you encourage her in her disobedience,' said the baron to his wife who, struck by this word as if by a blow, turned to stone.

'Rejecting an unjust command is not disobedience,' Ginevra replied.

'It cannot be unjust when it comes from your father's mouth, daughter! Why do you judge me? Is not the revulsion which I feel a warning from on high? I may be saving you from some misfortune.'

'The misfortune would be if he did not love me.'

'Him again!'

'Yes, again and always,' she replied. 'He is my life, my earthly goods, the thoughts in my mind. Even if I obeyed you, he would always be in my heart. If you forbid me to marry him, aren't you making me hate you?'

'You have stopped loving us,' Piombo said.

'No!' said Ginevra, shaking her head.

'Then forget him, remain faithful to us! After us… you know what I mean.'

'Father, are you trying to make me wish you dead?' cried Ginevra.

'I'll outlive you!' cried her father, at the height of exasperation. 'Children who do not honour their parents soon die.'

'All the more reason to marry soon and be happy!' she said.

For Piombo, this composure of hers, this ability to reason clearly, was the last straw. The blood rushed to his head, and his face turned purple. Ginevra shuddered. She flew to her father like a bird, perched on his knees, put her arms round his neck, stroked his hair, and exclaimed tenderly, 'Oh! yes, let me die first! I could not survive you, father, my dear father!'

'Oh my Ginevra, my mad Ginevra,' replied Piombo, all his anger melting away at this caress, like a block of ice in the sun.

'It was about time that you finished with all that,' said the baroness in a voice full of emotion.

'Poor mother!'

'*Ginevretta! Ma bella Ginevra!*'

49

And the father played with his daughter as if she were a child of six, he amused himself releasing the rippling tresses of her hair and bouncing her on his knee: there was a kind of madness in the expression of his love for her. Soon his daughter scolded him, kissed him and in jest tried to obtain permission for Louis to come to their house, but her father, equally in jest, refused. She sulked, asked him again, sulked some more; and by the end of the evening, she felt content at having imprinted on her father's heart both her love for Louis and the idea that they might marry soon. The next day, she said nothing more about her love. She went late to the studio and came back early; she was not only more affectionate towards her father than she had ever been, but full of gratitude, as if to thank him for what seemed to be his tacit consent to her marriage. For a long time that evening, she played the piano and sang, often exclaiming, 'This nocturne needs a man's voice!' She was Italian: that is all that needs to be said. After a week, her mother beckoned to her and, when she came, whispered in her ear, 'I've persuaded your father to receive him.'

'Oh mother! How happy you've made me!'

So that day Ginevra had the joy of returning home on Louis's arm. For the second time, the poor officer left his hiding place. The forceful appeals which Ginevra had made to the then Minister of War, the Duke de Feltre, had met with complete success. Louis had been reinstated on the list of reserve officers. It was an important step towards a better future. Having been forewarned by Ginevra of the difficulties awaiting him when he met the baron, the young man dared not confess his fear that Piombo would not like him. So courageous in adversity, so valiant on the battlefield, he trembled at the thought of entering the Piombos' drawing room. Ginevra sensed his trepidation, and this emotion, the basis of which lay in their happiness, was for her one more proof of his love.

'How pale you are!' she said to him, as they came to the front door of the mansion.

'Oh, Ginevra! If it were only my life that was at stake.'

Although Bartolomeo had been informed by his wife that the man whom Ginevra loved was to be officially presented to him, he did not go to meet him, but remained in the armchair where he usually sat, with a glacial expression.

'Father,' Ginevra said, 'I've brought you someone I'm sure you'll be pleased to see: Monsieur Louis, a soldier who fought beside the Emperor at Mont-Saint-Jean...'

The Baron de Piombo rose, glanced fleetingly at Louis, and said in a sardonic tone, 'Isn't Monsieur decorated?

'I no longer wear the Légion d'honneur,' replied Louis shyly, still humbly standing.

Ginevra, hurt by her father's rudeness, moved a chair forward. The officer's reply satisfied the baron. Madame Piombo, noting that her husband's eyebrows had resumed their normal position, said, to revive the conversation, 'Monsieur bears a remarkable resemblance to Nina Porta. A real Porta face, don't you think?'

'That's quite natural,' replied the young man, as Piombo's fiery eyes came to rest on him. 'Nina was my sister...'

'Are you Luigi Porta?' the old man asked.

'Yes.'

Bartolomeo di Piombo rose, tottered, and was obliged to lean on a chair. He looked at his wife. Elisa Piombo went to him, and the two old people left the drawing room in silence, arm in arm, abandoning their daughter with a kind of horror. Stunned, Luigi Porta looked at Ginevra, who had turned as white as a marble statue and was staring at the door through

51

which her father and mother had disappeared: there was something so solemn about this silent withdrawal that, for the first time perhaps, the feeling of fear entered her heart. She clasped her hands together and said in a voice so full of emotion that it could hardly be heard except by a lover, 'So much calamity in one word!'

'In the name of our love, what did I say?' asked Luigi Porta.

'My father,' she replied, 'has never spoken to me about our terrible history, and I was too young when I left Corsica to know it.'

'Is there a vendetta between us?' asked Luigi, trembling.

'Yes. When I questioned my mother, she told me that the Portas killed my brothers and burned our house down. My father slaughtered your whole family. How did you survive? He thought he'd tied you to the bedposts before he set fire to the house.'

'I don't know,' Luigi replied. 'At the age of six I was taken to Genoa, to live with an old man named Colonna. I wasn't told anything about my family. All I knew was that I was an orphan and penniless. This Colonna was like a father to me, and I bore his name until the day I joined the army. As I needed documents to prove who I was, old Colonna told me then that, weak as I was and not much more than a child, I had enemies. To escape them, he advised me to use only the name Luigi.'

'Go, go, Luigi!' cried Ginevra. 'But no, I must go with you. While you are in my father's house, you have nothing to fear; as soon as you leave, you must be very careful! You will be in great danger. My father has two Corsicans in his employ, and even if he does not threaten your life, they will.'

'Ginevra,' he said, 'is there such hatred between us?'

She smiled sadly and lowered her head. She soon raised it again with a kind of pride and said, 'Oh, Luigi, our feelings must be very pure and genuine if I am to have the strength to tread the path I have chosen. But we are talking about a happiness which must last all our lives, aren't we?'

Luigi's only response was a smile, and he squeezed Ginevra's hand. She understood that only true love could scorn commonplace protests at a time like this. The calm, conscientious way in which Luigi expressed his feelings was an indication of how strong they were, and how they would endure. The destiny of the two lovers was sealed at that moment. Ginevra foresaw a bitter struggle to come; but the idea of leaving Louis, an idea which may have floated in her soul, faded completely. She was his forever. With a sudden burst of energy, she led him out of the mansion, and did not leave him until they reached the house in which Servin had rented modest lodgings for him. By the time she returned to her father's house, she had assumed the kind of serenity that comes from a strong resolve: there was no change in her manner to indicate anxiety. She looked at her father and mother, who were ready for dinner, with eyes devoid of effrontery and full of gentleness. She could see that her old mother had wept, and for a moment the redness of those withered eyelids broke her heart, but she concealed her emotion. Piombo seemed to be in the grip of a pain so intense and concentrated that he could not betray it with any ordinary expression. Dinner was served, but none of them touched it. An aversion to food is one of the symptoms which reveal the great crises of the soul. All three rose from the table without anyone having uttered a word. When Ginevra was seated between her father and her mother in their large, dark, solemn drawing room, Piombo tried to speak, but his voice failed him; he tried to walk, and his strength failed him. He came back, sat down, and rang the bell.

'Pietro,' he said at last to the servant, 'light the fire, I feel cold.'

Ginevra trembled, and looked anxiously at her father. There was such distress on his face that he must have been in the grip of a terrible inner struggle. Ginevra knew the extent of the danger that threatened her, but she did not tremble; while the fleeting looks that Bartolomeo cast at his daughter seemed to indicate that he feared the intensity of her character, an intensity which was his own doing. Between them, everything had to be extreme. The likelihood of imminent change in the feelings of both father and daughter brought an expression of terror to the baroness' face.

'Ginevra, you are in love with your family's enemy,' said Piombo at last, without daring to look at his daughter.

'That's true,' she replied.

'You must choose between him and us. Our vendetta is part of our very being. Anyone who does not embrace my vengeance is no member of my family.'

'I have made my choice,' replied Ginevra, in a calm voice.

His daughter's tranquil tone deceived Bartolomeo. 'Oh my dear daughter!' cried the old man, and tears welled in his eyes, the first and only tears he had shed in his life.

'I will be his wife,' said Ginevra, curtly.

Bartolomeo had a kind of dizzy spell; but he recovered his composure and replied, 'This marriage will never take place in my lifetime, I'll never give my consent.' Ginevra remained silent. 'Don't you realise,' the baron went on, 'that Luigi is the son of the man who killed your brothers?'

'He was six years old when that happened,' she replied. 'How can he be guilty of the crime?'

'But he's a Porta!' cried Bartolomeo.

'Have I ever shared that hatred?' said Ginevra sharply. 'Did you raise me in the belief that a Porta was a monster? How was

I to know that anyone had survived of the family you killed? Isn't it natural that you should abandon your vendetta for the sake of my feelings?'

'A Porta!' said Piombo. 'If his father had found you in your bed that day, you would not be alive now, he would have taken your life a hundred times over.'

'That may be so,' she replied, 'but his son has given me more than life. Seeing Luigi is a joy I could not live without. Luigi has revealed the world of feelings to me. I may have seen faces even more handsome than his, but none has cast such a spell on me; I may have heard voices… no, no, none could be more melodious. Luigi loves me, he will be my husband.'

'Never, Ginevra,' Piombo said. 'I'd rather see you in your coffin.' He rose and started pacing about the drawing room, stopping a number of times in a way that betrayed the extent of his agitation. 'You think perhaps that you can bend my will?' he said at last. 'Think again: I do not want a Porta as my son-in-law. That is my final word. Let us never talk of this again. I am Bartolomeo di Piombo. Do you hear me, Ginevra?'

'Do you attach some mysterious meaning to those words?' she asked, coldly.

'They mean that I have a dagger, and that I do not fear the justice of men. We Corsicans answer to no one but God.'

'Very well!' said Ginevra, rising. 'I am Ginevra di Piombo, and I declare that in six months I will be the wife of Luigi Porta.' Then, after a terrifying pause, she went on, 'You are a tyrant, father.'

Bartolomeo clenched his fists and struck the marble mantelpiece. 'We are in Paris!' he said in a murmur.

He fell silent, folded his arms, dropped his head onto his chest and did not utter another word all evening. Having expressed her will, Ginevra assumed an extraordinary composure; she sat down at the piano, and sang and played a number of delightful pieces with a grace and feeling that indicated her complete independence of mind, thus scoring a victory over her father, whose brow gave no sign of softening. It was a tacit insult, and a cruel blow to the old man: at that moment, he was reaping one of the bitter fruits of the upbringing he had given his daughter. Respect is a barrier which protects both parents and children, sparing the former sorrow, and the latter remorse. The next day Ginevra, trying to leave the house at the usual hour to go to the studio, found the front door locked; but she soon found a means to inform Luigi Porta of her father's stern measures. She wrote the young officer a letter and had it delivered for her by a chambermaid who could not read. For five days the two lovers were able to correspond, thanks to the kind of subterfuge it is always possible to concoct at the age of twenty. Father and daughter rarely spoke to each other. Both felt, deep in their hearts, a degree of hatred, which made them suffer, but proudly and in silence. Acknowledging how strong were the ties of love that bound them to one another, they attempted to sunder them, but were unable to do so. No gentle thoughts any longer brightened Bartolomeo's stern features as he contemplated his Ginevra, while there was something inflexible about her when she looked at her father, a constant reproach on her innocent brow; although she had happy thoughts, remorse sometimes seemed to dull her eyes. It was not difficult to sense that she would never be able to enjoy in peace a happiness which made her parents unhappy. In both Bartolomeo and his daughter, all the indecisiveness caused by the native goodness of their souls had nevertheless to give way to the pride and rancour peculiar to Corsicans. They encouraged one another in their anger and closed their eyes to the future. Perhaps they both flattered themselves that one would yield to the other.

On Ginevra's birthday, her mother, in despair at this increasingly serious rift, thought that she might be able to reconcile father and daughter thanks to the memories aroused by this anniversary. All three gathered in Bartolomeo's bedroom. Ginevra guessed her mother's intentions from the hesitation clearly visible on her face, and smiled sadly. At that moment, a servant announced two notaries, who entered accompanied by several witnesses. Bartolomeo stared at these men, whose cold, formal faces seemed like an offence to souls as passionate as those of the three principal actors of this scene. The old man turned anxiously to his daughter, and saw on her face a smile of triumph which made him suspect some disaster; but he chose, like a savage, to remain deceptively still, looking at the two notaries with a kind of calm curiosity. The strangers sat down after being invited to do so by a gesture from the old man.

'I take it that Monsieur is the Baron de Piombo?' said the older of the notaries.

Bartolomeo bowed. The notary made a slight movement with his head, looked at Ginevra with a crafty expression, as if surprising a debtor, took out his snuffbox, opened it, and took a pinch of snuff, searching as he did so for the opening words of his speech; then, as he spoke, he paused constantly (an oratorical device which will be very imperfectly represented here by the sign –).

'Monsieur,' he said, 'I am Monsieur Roguin, your daughter's notary, and we have come – my colleague and myself – to fulfil the wishes of the law and – to put an end to the divisions which – appear to have arisen – between you and your daughter – concerning – her marriage – to Monsieur Luigi Porta.'

Maître Roguin probably thought this pedantically spouted sentence too beautiful to be understood immediately, and he stopped and looked at Bartolomeo with an expression peculiar to those involved with business, an expression halfway between servility and familiarity. Accustomed to feigning a great deal of interest in the people to whom they speak, notaries always end up with their faces distorted by a grimace which they put on and take off as if it were their official pallium. This mask of benevolence, the mechanism of which is so easy to grasp, so irritated Bartolomeo that he had to use all his self-control not to throw Monsieur Roguin out of the window. An angry expression crept into his features, and on seeing it the notary said to himself, 'I'm having an effect!'

'But,' he went on in a honeyed voice, 'Monsieur le Baron, at times like this, our mission is always an essentially conciliatory one at first. – Please be so kind, therefore, as to hear me out. – It is evident that Mademoiselle Ginevra Piombo – has today reached the age – at which it is merely necessary to make a legal declaration in order to be able to proceed with the celebration of a marriage – even when the parents withhold their consent. Now – it is customary in families – who enjoy a certain esteem – who are part of society – who retain some dignity – to whom, last but not least, it is important not to reveal their secret divisions in public – and who in addition have no wish to do harm to themselves by casting their disapproval over the future of two young people – (for that would indeed be to harm themselves!) – it is customary – as I say – among these respectable families – not to allow such declarations to remain – since such declarations bear witness – to a division which eventually – ceases. – Once a young lady has recourse to legal declarations, she announces her intentions in such a way that a father and – a mother,' he added turning to the baroness, 'can never hope to see her follow their advice. Parental objections being first rendered null and void – by such declarations – then invalidated by law, it is acknowledged that any sensible man, having made a final admonition to his child, must give her the freedom to – '

Realising that he could talk like this for two hours without obtaining any response, Monsieur Roguin broke off, much struck in addition by the demeanour of the man he was trying to win over. An extraordinary transformation had taken place on Bartolomeo's face: his distorted features gave him an air of indefinable cruelty, and the look he cast on the notary was as fierce as that of a tiger. The baroness remained silent and passive. Ginevra waited, calm and resolute: aware that the notary's voice was more powerful than her own, she seemed to have decided to remain silent. When Roguin stopped speaking, the scene became so terrifying that the witnesses trembled: never before, perhaps, had they encountered such a silence. The notaries looked at each other as if to confer. They stood up and walked over to the window.

'Have you ever come across clients like these?' Roguin asked his colleague.

'We won't get anything from them,' replied the younger man. 'If I were in your place, I'd just read the document and leave it at that. The old man's no laughing matter, he's a hot-tempered fellow, and you'll gain nothing by trying to argue with him…'

Monsieur Roguin proceeded to read out a previously pre-pared statement from a stamped sheet of paper, and coldly asked Bartolomeo for his response.

'Are there laws in France, then, which usurp a father's authority?' the baron asked.

'Monsieur – ' began Roguin in his honeyed voice.

'Which tear a daughter from her father?'

'Monsieur – '

'Which deprive an old man of his last consolation?'

'Monsieur, your daughter only belongs to you insofar as – '

'Which kill him?'

'Monsieur, if you'll allow me?'

Nothing is more dreadful than the composure, the dry rationality, of a notary in the midst of the passionate scenes in which they are usually called upon to intervene. The faces Piombo saw before him seemed to him to have come straight from hell, and when the calm, almost fluty voice of his poor antagonist uttered that deadly 'If you'll allow me?' his cold, concentrated rage knew no bounds. He seized a long dagger hanging from a nail above the mantelpiece and hurled himself at his daughter. The younger of the two notaries and one of the witnesses threw themselves between him and Ginevra; but Bartolomeo knocked both men back violently, his red face and fiery eyes looking more fearsome than the gleam of the dagger. When Ginevra found herself face to face with her father, she looked straight at him with a triumphant air, walked slowly towards him and knelt.

'No! no! I can't!' he said, throwing his weapon from him with such force that it embedded itself in the wood panelling.

'Have mercy!' said Ginevra. 'You can't bring yourself to put me to death, and yet you refuse me life. Oh, father, I have never loved you so much. Grant me Luigi! I am asking for your consent on my knees: a daughter can humiliate herself before her father. My Luigi, or I die.'

The intense emotion that was choking her prevented her from continuing, but although her voice failed her, her convulsive movements indicated clearly enough that this was now a matter of life and death. Bartolomeo pushed her away harshly.

'Go,' he said. 'The wife of Luigi Porta could never be a Piombo. I no longer have a daughter! I don't have the strength to curse you; but I abandon you, and you no longer have a father. My Ginevra Piombo is buried here,' he cried in a deep voice, clutching his heart. 'So go, wretched girl,' he went on after a moment's silence, 'go, and never show your face here again.' Then he took Ginevra by the arm, and led her silently out of the house.

'Luigi,' cried Ginevra, as she entered the young officer's humble apartment, 'my Luigi, the only fortune we have is our love.'

'Then we are richer than any monarch on earth,' he replied.

'My father and mother have abandoned me,' she said, with deep melancholy.

'I will love you for them.'

'Then we will be happy?' she cried with a gaiety about which there was something terrifying.

'Forever,' he replied, clasping her to his breast.

The day after Ginevra left her father's house, she went to see Madame Servin and asked her for shelter and protection until the time when she would be legally able to marry Luigi Porta. There now began her apprenticeship in those sorrows which the world strews before those who do not follow its customs. Greatly distressed by the harm which Ginevra's adventure had caused her husband, Madame Servin received the fugitive coldly, and informed her in politely circumspect words that she was not to count on her support. Too proud to insist, but surprised by a selfishness to which she was not accustomed, Ginevra took up residence in the closest furnished lodgings to the house where Luigi was staying. Every day, he would come and sit at her feet, and the youthfulness of his love, the purity of his words, would dispel the clouds which the baron's disapproval had caused to gather on his banished daughter's brow. He would paint such a beautiful picture of their future that she would end by smiling, even though she could never forget her parents' harshness.

One morning, the maid at her lodgings brought Ginevra several trunks containing fabrics, linen, and a mass of things necessary to a young woman who is setting up house. She recognised in this consignment the provident kindness of a mother, for, in examining these gifts, she found a purse in which the baroness had put the sum which belonged to her daughter, as well as her own savings. The money was accompanied by a letter in which her mother beseeched her to abandon her disastrous marriage plans before it was too late. She had had to take extraordinary precautions, she wrote, to send Ginevra even this meagre aid, and she begged her not to accuse her of being hard-hearted if she subsequently neglected her, for she feared that she would be unable to help her again. She blessed her, hoped that she would find happiness in this regrettable marriage if she persisted with it, and assured her that she was thinking only of her beloved daughter. At this point in the letter, several words had been obliterated by tears.

'Oh, mother!' cried Ginevra, melting. She wished that she could see her, throw herself at her knees, breath the salutary air of her father's house. She was about to rush out when Luigi entered; she looked at him, and her filial love vanished away, her tears dried up: she did not feel strong enough to abandon this child, who was so unhappy and so loving. To be the only hope of a noble creature, to love him and abandon him... such a sacrifice is a betrayal of which young souls are incapable. Generously, Ginevra buried her sorrow deep in her soul.

At last the wedding day arrived, and Ginevra found herself alone. Luigi had taken advantage of the fact that she was getting dressed to go and find the witnesses needed to sign their wedding certificate. These witnesses were good people. One, a former sergeant of hussars who now rented out carriages and owned a small fleet of fiacres, had served in the army with Luigi and had contracted the kind of obligations towards him which can never fade from the heart of an honest man. The other, a builder, was the owner of the house where the bride and groom were to lodge. Each of them found a friend to accompany him, then all four came with Luigi to fetch the bride. Unaccustomed to social posturing, and seeing the service they were performing for Luigi as something very simple, these people had dressed decently but unostentatiously, and there was nothing to indicate that this was a joyful wedding procession. Ginevra herself dressed very simply in accordance with her financial situation; but there was something so noble and so imposing about her beauty that, as soon as they saw her, words died on the lips of the witnesses, and they felt obliged to compliment her. They greeted her respectfully, she curtsied, and then they looked at her in silence, unable to do anything other than gaze at her in admiration. This reserve threw a chill over them. Joy can only burst forth among people who feel equal. As luck would have it, then, all was sombre and grave around the bride and groom, and nothing reflected their happiness. The church and the town hall were not very far from Ginevra's lodgings. The young couple, followed by the four witnesses which the law demanded, decided to go there on foot, thus divesting this great social event of all pomp. In the courtyard of the town hall, they found a host of carriages, which indicated that a large number of people were already there. They went upstairs and came to a large room where the bridal couples whose joy was planned for that day were waiting somewhat impatiently for the local mayor. Ginevra sat down beside Luigi at the end of a long bench. As there were not enough seats, their witnesses remained standing. There were two brides pompously dressed in white, laden with ribbons, lace and pearls, and crowned with bouquets of orange blossom whose satin-smooth buds shook beneath their veils, surrounded by their happy families, and accompanied by their mothers, whom they looked at with a mixture of satisfaction and timidity; all eyes reflected their happiness, and every face seemed to lavish blessings on them. The fathers, the witnesses, the brothers, the sisters, came and went like a swarm of insects playing in a ray of sunlight which is about to disappear. They all seemed to understand the value of this fleeting moment in life when the heart finds itself between two hopes: the wishes of the past and the promises of the future. Ginevra felt her heart swell at the sight, and she squeezed Luigi's arm. He looked at her, his eyes filling with tears: now more than ever he understood how much his Ginevra was sacrificing for him. These precious tears made her forget the fact that she had been abandoned. Love scattered treasures of light over the two lovers, who had eyes only for each other in the midst of this commotion: there they were, alone in that crowd, as they were to be in life. Their witnesses, indifferent to the ceremony, were happily chatting away about their respective businesses.

'Oats are quite expensive,' the sergeant was saying to the builder.

'Not yet as expensive as plaster, relatively speaking,' replied the builder.

And they went for a walk about the room.

'They certainly take their time here!' exclaimed the builder, putting his big silver watch back in his pocket.

Luigi and Ginevra, huddled close together, seemed to have become one and the same person. A poet would surely have admired these two heads united by a single feeling, both equally melancholy and silent in the presence of the two wedding parties buzzing around them, four boisterous families glittering with diamonds and flowers, whose gaiety had something fleeting about it. All the joy these noisy, opulent groups displayed on the outside Luigi and Ginevra buried deep in their hearts. On one side, the vulgar din of pleasure; on the other, the delicate silence of joyful souls: heaven and earth. But Ginevra was not entirely free of a woman's weakness – a superstitious Italian woman's, indeed – and, with a shudder, she saw an omen in this contrast, an omen which left her with a feeling of terror deep within her that was just as invincible as her love. All at once, an employee in the livery of the city opened a double door, and silence fell. His voice echoed like a dog's yapping as he called out the names of Monsieur Luigi da Porta and Mademoiselle Ginevra di Piombo. This caused some embarrassment to the bride and groom. The name Piombo was famous enough to draw the spectators' attention, and they looked around them for a wedding party which they assumed would be lavish. Ginevra rose, her proud, fierce look impressing the crowd, gave her arm to Luigi, and stepped forward resolutely, followed by her witnesses. A rising murmur of surprise, a general whispering, told Ginevra that the world was demanding an explanation for her parents' absence: her father's curse seemed to be pursuing her.

'Wait for the families,' said the mayor to the employee, who had already started on the reading of the certificate.

'The father and the mother object,' replied the secretary, phlegmatically.

'On both sides?' the mayor asked.

'The bridegroom is an orphan.'

'Where are the witnesses?'

'Here they are,' replied the secretary, pointing to the four men who stood with their arms folded, as silent and motionless as statues.

'But if there is an objection – ' said the mayor.

'The declarations have been legally made,' retorted the secretary, standing up and handing the mayor the papers appended to the marriage certificate.

There was something about this bureaucratic discussion which threw a stain on proceedings, containing as it did a whole history in a few words. The terrible hatred of the Portas and the Piombos was inscribed on a page of the public record, just as the annals of a nation are sometimes carved on a gravestone in a few lines, or even in one word: Robespierre or Napoleon. Ginevra was trembling. Like the dove crossing the seas, able only to alight on the ark, her gaze could only find shelter in Luigi's eyes, for everything was sad and cold around her. The mayor had a stern, reproving air, and his secretary was looking at the bride and groom with malevolent curiosity. Nothing seemed less like a celebration. Like all things in human life, when they are stripped of their trappings, it was a simple event in itself, but immense in thought. After a few questions to which the bride and groom replied, after a few words muttered by the mayor, and after the appending of their signatures to the register, Luigi and Ginevra were joined in marriage. The two young Corsicans, whose union contained all the poetry with which the genius depicted that of Romeo and Juliet, walked out between two lines of happy parents to which they did not belong, and who were becoming quite impatient at the delay caused them by this wedding that seemed so sad. When Ginevra found herself in the courtyard of the town hall, beneath the open sky, a sigh escaped her breast.

'Will a whole lifetime of care and love be enough to re-cognise my Ginevra's courage and tenderness?' said Luigi.

At these words, accompanied by tears of joy, the bride forgot all her woes – for it had grieved her to appear before the world to demand a happiness which her family refused to sanction.

'Why must men come between us?' she said, with an inno-cence that delighted Luigi.

Pleasure made the bride and groom feel lighter. They did not see the sky, or the earth, or the houses, and flew to the church as if on wings. At last, they reached a dark little chapel, where an old priest celebrated their union at an unadorned altar. There, as in the town hall, they were surrounded by the two other wedding parties, which seemed to be persecuting them with their brilliance. The church, full of friends and rela-tives, echoed to the noise made by the coaches, the beadles, the vergers and the priests. Altars glittered with every ecclesi-astical luxury; the crowns of orange blossom which adorned the statues of the Virgin seemed to be new. There was a riot of flowers, scents, flashing candles, velvet cushions embroidered in gold. God Himself appeared to smile on this short-lived joy. When the time came to hold above the heads of Luigi and Ginevra that symbol of everlasting union, that yoke of soft, shiny white satin, light for some, leaden for most, the priest looked about for the young boys who usually performed this joyful task, but in vain: two of the witnesses took their place. The priest hastily lectured the bride and groom on the perils of life and the duties they would one day teach their children – incidentally slipping in an indirect reproach on the absence of Ginevra's parents – then, after uniting them before God, as the mayor had united them before the law, he finished the service and left them.

'God bless them!' said Sergeant Vergniaud to the builder at the door of the church. 'Never were two people more clearly meant for each other. That girl's parents are idiots. I don't know a braver soldier than Colonel Louis! If everyone had behaved like him, you-know-who would still be here.'

The soldier's blessing, the only one they received that day, was like balm to Ginevra's heart.

They parted with a handshake, and Luigi thanked his landlord cordially.

'Farewell, my good man,' said Luigi to the sergeant, 'and thank you.'

'At your service, colonel. My body and soul, my horses and carriages, everything I have is yours.'

'How he loves him!' said Ginevra.

Luigi quickly led his bride to the house in which they were going to live. They soon came to their modest apartment; and there, when the door was closed behind them, Luigi took his wife in his arms and cried, 'Oh my Ginevra! For now you are mine, here is the true celebration. Here,' he went on, 'everything will smile on us.'

Together they walked through the three rooms which comprised their living quarters. The first room was a combined drawing room and dining room. On the right was a bedroom, on the left a large study which Luigi had made ready for his dear wife and where she found the easels, the paint box, the plaster casts, the models, the dummies, the canvases, the portfolios, in other words, all that an artist could need.

'So this is where I'll work,' she said, with a childlike expression. She looked for a long time at the curtains and the furniture, constantly turning to Luigi to thank him, for there was a kind of magnificence in this little room: a bookcase contained Ginevra's favourite books, and at the far end stood a piano. She sat down on a divan, drew Luigi to her, and squeezed his hand. 'You have good taste,' she said in a tender voice.

'Your words make me very happy,' he said.

'But let's see everything,' said Ginevra, for Luigi had kept the details of this retreat a mystery.

They went next to the bedroom, which was as cool and white as a virgin.

'Let's go out!' said Luigi, laughing.

'But I want to see everything.' And the imperious Ginevra inspected the furnishings with all the care and attention of an antiquary examining a medal, touching the silks and scrutinising everything with the innocent contentment of a young bride laying out the riches of her dowry. 'We're spending too much too soon,' she said, with a mixture of joy and despondency.

'It's true!' replied Luigi. 'All I am still owed as a soldier is here. I mortgaged it to a good man named Gigonnet.'

'Why?' Ginevra asked in a reproachful tone, although there was a secret satisfaction behind it. 'Do you think I would be less happy in a garret? But,' she went on, 'all this is really nice, and it's ours.' Luigi was looking at her with such enthusiasm that she lowered her eyes and said, 'Let's go and see the rest.'

Above these three rooms, beneath the roof, there was a study for Luigi, a kitchen and a maid's room. Ginevra was pleased with her little domain, although the view was limited by the large wall of a neighbouring house, and the only daylight came from a dark courtyard. But the two lovers' hearts were so happy, and hope cast the future in such a rosy light, that they preferred to see only delightful images in their mysterious refuge. There they were, in the midst of this vast house, lost in the immensity of Paris, like two pearls in their oyster, deep in the sea: for anyone else it would have been a prison, for them it was a paradise. The first days of their union were given over to love. Unable to resist the spell of their own passion, they could not bring themselves to get down to work immediately. Luigi would lie for hours on end at his wife's feet, admiring the colour of her hair, the sweep of her brow, her ravishing eyes, the purity and whiteness of the two arches beneath which they turned slowly, expressing the happiness of requited love. Ginevra would caress her Luigi's hair, never tiring of gazing on what she called his *beltà folgorante*, the delicacy of his features; always enchanted by the nobility of his manners, as she always enchanted him with the grace of hers. They would play like children with trifles, these trifles always led them back to their passion, and they only ceased their games to fall into daydreaming, into a state of *far niente*. A melody sung by Ginevra reminded them of the sweet subtleties of their love. Then, uniting their steps as they had united their souls, they explored the countryside, seeing their love reflected everywhere, in the flowers, in the sky, in the fiery colours of the setting sun; they saw it even on the wayward clouds clashing in the air. No one day was like another: their love continued growing because it was true. They had tested each other in these few days, and had instinctively recognised that their souls were the kind whose inexhaustible riches seem always to promise fresh pleasures in the future. This was love in all its innocence, with its endless chats, its unfinished sentences, its long silences, its oriental repose and its passion. Luigi and Ginevra had understood everything about love. Is not love like the sea which, seen superficially or hastily, is accused of monotony by commonplace souls, while the lucky few can spend their whole lives gazing at it in admiration, constantly delighted by the changing phenomena they find in it?

Nevertheless, one day, practical thoughts drew the young couple from their Eden: it had become necessary to work in order to live. Ginevra, who had a particular talent for imitating old paintings, began making copies, and found customers among the dealers in second-hand goods. For his part, Luigi looked very actively for work, but it was very difficult for a young officer, whose one talent was for military tactics, to find employment in Paris.

At last, wearied one day by his vain efforts, despair in his soul at the knowledge that the burden of their existence fell entirely on Ginevra, he thought of turning his fine handwriting to his advantage. Taking his wife's determination as an example, he applied to the solicitors, notaries and lawyers of Paris. His situation and the openness of his manners worked in his favour, and he obtained so many commissions that he was obliged to take on a number of young people to help him. Gradually he undertook clerical work on a large scale. With what he earned, and the prices Ginevra commanded, the young couple were at last able to lead a comfortable life, a fact in which they took pride, for it had come about as a result of their own industry. This was the best time of their lives. The days passed rapidly, divided between their work and the joys of love. In the evening, after a good day's work, they were happy to meet in Ginevra's cell. Music consoled them for their exhaustion. Never once did a melancholy expression darken Ginevra's features, never once did she allow herself to complain. She always managed to greet her Luigi with a smile on her lips and a sparkle in her eyes. Both entertained one overriding thought which would have made them find pleasure in the roughest work: Ginevra told herself that she was working for Luigi, and Luigi that he was working for Ginevra. Sometimes, when her husband was absent, Ginevra would dream of how perfectly happy she would have been if this life filled with love had been lived in the presence of her father and mother, and then she would fall into a deep melancholy, overcome with remorse; dark images passed like shadows through her imagination: she would see her old father alone, or her mother weeping in the evening and hiding her tears from the unyielding Piombo; their two solemn white heads would suddenly loom up before her, and it seemed to her that she would never see them again except in the fantastic light of memory. This idea haunted her like a premonition. She marked the anniversary of her wedding by giving her husband a portrait he had often desired: that of his Ginevra. Never before had she produced anything so remarkable. Not only was it a perfect likeness, but the radiance of her beauty, the purity of her feelings, the happiness of love, were rendered with a kind of magic. The masterpiece was unveiled. They lived comfortably for another year. The story of their life can be summed up in three words: *They were happy*. In other words, nothing deserving of comment befell them.

At the beginning of the winter of 1819, the picture dealers asked Ginevra to give them something other than copies, which they were no longer able to sell at a profit due to strong competition. She realised that she had been wrong not to practise painting genre subjects, which would have made her reputation. She undertook to produce portraits, but had to compete against a host of artists even less rich than she was. Nevertheless, as Luigi and Ginevra had amassed some money, they did not despair of the future. By the end of that same winter, Luigi was working without respite. He too had to struggle against competitors: the prices paid for clerical work had fallen so much that he could no longer afford to employ anyone, and he found himself forced to devote more time than previously to his labour in order to make the same amount of money. His wife had finished several paintings which were not without merit, but the dealers were barely even buying those of reputable artists. Even though Ginevra offered them for next to nothing, she was unable to sell them. There was something dreadful about the situation of this household: while the souls of the two spouses knew no bounds to their happiness and love overwhelmed them with its treasures, Poverty rose like a skeleton amid this harvest of pleasure. They concealed their anxieties from one another. Whenever Ginevra would feel herself close to tears at the sight of her Luigi suffering, she would smother him with caresses. In the same way, Luigi kept a dark sorrow deep in his heart while expressing the tenderest love to Ginevra. They sought compensation for their ills in the elation of their feelings, and their words, their joys, their games were tinged with a kind of frenzy. They were afraid of the future. What feeling can compare in strength with a passion which must cease the next day, snuffed out by death or necessity? Whenever they spoke of their situation, they felt the need to deceive one another, and both grasped at the slightest hope with equal fervour. One night, Ginevra woke to find Luigi gone, and rose from the bed in panic. A dim light reflected on the dark wall of the little courtyard revealed to her that her husband had been working during the night. Luigi would always wait until his wife was asleep before going upstairs to his study. Four o'clock sounded, and Ginevra went back to bed and pretended to sleep. Luigi returned, overcome with fatigue, and Ginevra looked sadly at that handsome face on which work and cares had already stamped a few lines.

'It's because of me that he spends his nights writing,' she said, weeping.

Then a thought came to her, and her tears ceased. She would do the same as Luigi. That very day she went to see a rich dealer in prints, and with the help of a letter of recommendation from Élie Magus, who had bought paintings from her in the past, she obtained colouring work. By day, she painted and attended to household chores; then when night came, she would colour engravings. These two creatures enamoured of love only entered the marriage bed to leave it. Both pretended to sleep, and no sooner had one of them deceived the other than he or she would go. One night, Luigi, giving way beneath the weight of work, and feeling feverish, opened the skylight of his study to breathe the pure air of morning and shake off his sorrows. Looking down, he saw the light cast on the wall by Ginevra's lamp. Guessing everything, he went softly downstairs, and surprised his wife in the middle of her studio, illuminating engravings.

'Oh, Ginevra!' he burst out.

She gave a start on her chair and turned red.

'Could I sleep while you were tiring yourself out?' she said.

'But I alone have the right to work like this.'

'Can I remain idle,' she replied, her eyes filling with tears, 'when I know that every piece of bread costs us almost a drop of your blood? I would die if I did not add my efforts to yours. Shouldn't we share everything, pleasures and pains?'

'She's cold,' cried Luigi in despair. 'Pull your shawl over your chest, my Ginevra, the night is damp and cold.'

They went and stood by the window. Ginevra laid her head on her beloved's chest while he held her around the waist, and the two of them, shrouded in a deep silence, looked at the sky as it slowly brightened with the dawn. Grey clouds scurried past, and the east became lighter and lighter.

'You see?' said Ginevra. 'It's an omen. We will be happy.'

'Yes, in heaven,' replied Luigi with a bitter smile. 'Oh, Ginevra! You deserved all the treasures on earth...'

'I have your heart,' she said, joyfully.

'Oh, I'm not complaining,' he went on, clasping her to him. And he covered her face with kisses, that delicate face which was beginning to lose the freshness of youth, but which was still so tender, so gentle in its expression that he could never see it without finding consolation.

'How quiet it is!' Ginevra said. 'My dear, it's such a pleasure, staying awake. The majesty of the night is really contagious, it impresses, it inspires. There's a kind of power in the thought that everything is asleep and I am still awake.'

'Oh, my Ginevra! I've always known that your soul was gracious and sensitive! But it's dawn now, come to bed.'

'I will,' she replied, 'as long as I don't have to sleep alone. I suffered so much last night when I realised that my Luigi was up and I wasn't!'

For a time, the courage with which these two young people struggled against misfortune had its reward. Then something happened, an event which usually crowns the happiness of a household but in their case was to prove disastrous: Ginevra gave birth to a son who, to use a popular expression, was as beautiful as the daylight. Her maternal feelings gave the young woman new strength. Luigi borrowed in order to meet the expenses of Ginevra's confinement. At first, therefore, she was not fully aware of the difficulty of her situation, and the two spouses gave themselves wholeheartedly to the joy of raising a child. It was to be their last joy. Like two swimmers who unite their efforts to beat the current, the two Corsicans at first struggled courageously; but sometimes they succumbed to an apathy similar to those sleeps which precede death; and before long they found themselves obliged to sell their jewels.

Poverty appeared suddenly, not as a hideous figure, but simply dressed, and almost bearable; there was nothing terrifying about its voice, it brought with it no despair, no ghosts, no rags; but it wiped out the memory and habits of their comfortable life; it wore down their reserves of pride. Then came Misery in all its horror, heedless of being in rags and tatters, trampling on all human feeling. Seven or eight months after the birth of little Bartolomeo, it would have been hard to recognise in the mother suckling this puny child the original of the admirable portrait, the only ornament of a bare room. Without a fire during a harsh winter, Ginevra saw the graceful contours of her face slowly disappear, her cheeks turned as white as porcelain, and her eyes grew pale as if the wellspring of life were running dry within her. Seeing her child grow thin and colourless, she felt only his suffering. Luigi could no longer bear to smile at his son.

'I've been all over Paris,' he would say in a subdued voice, 'but I don't know anyone, and how can I dare ask strangers? Vergniaud, my old sergeant, is implicated in a conspiracy, and has been put in prison, and besides, he's already lent me everything he had. As for our landlord, he hasn't asked us for anything for a year.'

'But we don't need anything,' replied Ginevra softly, assuming a calm air.

'Every day that arrives brings one more problem,' Luigi went on, in terror.

Luigi took all Ginevra's paintings, including the portrait, and several pieces of furniture which the couple could do without, and sold them all for next to nothing. The money he obtained prolonged the couple's agony for a short while. At this terrible time, Ginevra demonstrated the sublimity of her character and the extent of her resignation. She bore her pains stoically; her energetic soul sustained her against all ills, she worked with an unsteady hand beside her dying son, by some miracle did all the household chores, and coped with everything. She was even happy whenever Luigi smiled in surprise at the sight of the cleanliness which, thanks to her, prevailed in the one room where they had taken refuge.

'My dear, I've kept you this piece of bread,' she said to him one evening when he came home tired.

'And you?'

'I've eaten, dear Luigi, I don't need anything.'

It was less the words than the gentle expression on her face which urged him to accept a piece of food of which she was depriving herself. Luigi kissed her with the kind of desperate kiss which friends gave one another in 1793 as they mounted the scaffold together. At such supreme moments, two people see into each other's hearts. Thus the unfortunate Luigi, realising suddenly that his wife had eaten nothing, shared the fever which was consuming her. He shuddered, and went out on the pretext of having urgent business, for he would have preferred to take the strongest poison, rather than avoid death by eating the last piece of bread in the house. He began wandering the streets of Paris, surrounded by the most brilliant carriages, in the midst of that insulting luxury that is everywhere in evidence; he hurried past the shops of the moneychangers where gold glitters. Finally, he resolved to sell himself: he would offer his services as a military reserve, hoping that this sacrifice would save Ginevra, and that, during his absence, she might be able to come back into favour with Bartolomeo. He therefore went to see one of those men who trade in people, and felt a kind of joy when he recognised him as a former officer of the Imperial Guard.

'I haven't eaten for two days,' he said slowly, in a weak voice. 'My wife is dying of hunger, and never complains, she would die with a smile on her face, I think. I beg you, comrade,' he went on, with a bitter smile, 'buy me in advance, I'm strong, I'm no longer in the service, and I...'

The officer gave some money to Luigi as an advance on the sum he undertook to procure for him. Once he had a few gold coins in his hand, the poor wretch gave a convulsive laugh, and set off for home as fast as he could, panting and crying from time to time, 'Ginevra! My Ginevra!' Night was starting to fall by the time he reached home. He entered very quietly, so as not to startle his wife, who had been weak when he had left. The last rays of the sun entering through the skylight came to rest on Ginevra's face as she slept on a chair, holding her child to her breast.

'Wake up, my soul,' he said, without noticing the child's posture or its unearthly sheen.

Hearing his voice, the poor mother opened her eyes, met Luigi's gaze, and smiled. Luigi let out a cry of horror: his wife seemed almost mad, and he could barely recognise her. In a wild burst of energy, he showed her the money, and she began to laugh mechanically. Suddenly she cried out in a ghastly voice, 'Louis! The child is cold.' She looked at her son and fainted, for little Barthélemy was dead. Luigi took his wife in his arms, but made no attempt to remove the child, whom she was hugging to her with a strength that was incomprehensible. He laid her on the bed and went out to call for help.

'Oh, my God!' he said to his landlord, meeting him on the staircase. 'I have money, and my child has died of starvation, his mother is dying, help us!'

He returned in despair to his wife, leaving the honest builder and several neighbours to gather whatever they could find to relieve a terrible situation they had not even suspected, so carefully had the two Corsicans, in their pride, concealed it from them. Luigi had thrown his money on the floor, and had knelt beside the bed where his wife lay.

'Father!' cried Ginevra in her delirium. 'Take care of my son who bears your name!'

'Hush now, my angel!' Luigi said, embracing her. 'There are happy days awaiting us.'

This voice and this caress restored a little calm to her.

'Oh my Louis!' she said, looking at him extremely closely. 'Listen carefully. I know that I am dying. It's only natural that I should die, I've been suffering too much, and besides, great happiness such as I have had must be paid for. Yes, my Luigi, don't be sad. I've been so happy that if I were to have my life over again, I would gladly accept our destiny. I am a bad mother: I'll miss you even more than I'll miss my child. My child,' she repeated in a deep voice. Two tears fell from her dying eyes, and suddenly she hugged the corpse she had been unable to warm. 'Give my hair to my father, in memory of his Ginevra,' she went on. 'Make sure you tell him I have never blamed him….' Her head dropped onto her husband's arm.

'No, you can't die,' Luigi cried, 'the doctor's on his way. We have bread. Your father will take you back into his favour. We'll be prosperous again. Stay with us, angel of beauty!'

But that loyal, loving heart was growing cold. Ginevra instinctively turned her eyes towards the man she loved, although she was no longer aware of anything: confused images went through her mind, which had almost lost all memory of earth. She knew that Luigi was there, for she was squeezing his ice-cold hand ever harder, as if trying to cling to a precipice from which she felt as though she were about to fall.

'My dear,' she said at last, 'you're cold, I'll warm you.'

She tried to place her husband's hand on her heart, but expired before she could do so. Two doctors, a priest and some neighbours arrived at that moment, bringing all that was needed to save the two spouses and ease their despair. They entered noisily at first, but by the time they were all inside, a terrible silence had fallen in the room.

While this scene was taking place, Bartolomeo and his wife were sitting in their ancient armchairs, each at a corner of the vast hearth in which a blazing fire barely warmed the immense drawing room of their mansion. The clock was striking midnight. It was a long time since the old couple had been able to sleep. At that moment, they were as silent as two old people in their second childhood, who look at everything and see nothing. Their drawing room, deserted but full of memories, was dimly lit by a single lamp that had almost died. Without the sparkling flames in the hearth, they would have been in complete darkness. A friend of theirs had just left, and the chair on which he had been sitting during his visit stood between them. Piombo had already thrown more than one glance at this chair, and these glances, heavy with thoughts, followed one another like pangs of remorse, for the empty chair had been Ginevra's. Elisa Piombo was watching the expressions crossing her husband's pale face. Although she was accustomed to guessing what he felt from the changes in his features, these expressions were alternately so threatening and so melancholy that she felt as though his soul had become incomprehensible to her.

Was Bartolomeo succumbing to the powerful memories aroused by that chair? Was he shocked to see that it had been used to seat a stranger for the first time since his daughter's departure? Had the hour of his clemency, that hour so long awaited in vain, arrived at last?

One after the other, these reflections troubled Elisa Piombo's heart. For a moment, her husband's countenance became so terrible that she trembled at the thought that she had dared to employ such a simple stratagem to create the opportunity to talk about Ginevra. At that moment, the wind blew the snowflakes so violently from the shutters that the two old people could hear them rustling. Ginevra's mother lowered her head to hide her tears from her husband. All at once, a sigh emerged from the old man's chest. His wife looked at him, and saw how downcast he was. For only the second time in three years, she ventured to talk to him of his daughter.

'What if Ginevra is cold?' she said softly. Piombo shuddered. 'She may be hungry,' she went on. A tear fell from the baron's eye. 'She has a child, and can't feed him, her milk has dried up,' his wife continued rapidly, desperately.

'Let her come!' Piombo cried. 'Let her come! Oh, my dear child! You have defeated me.'

The mother rose as if to go and fetch her daughter. At that moment, the door opened with a crash, and a man whose face seemed no longer human suddenly appeared before them.

'Dead!' he said. 'Our two families were destined to exterminate one another, for here is all that remains of her.' And he placed Ginevra's long black hair on a table.

The two old people shuddered as if they had been struck by lightning, and when they looked again, Luigi seemed to have gone.

Then Bartolomeo looked down at the floor. 'He's saved us having to shoot him,' he said, slowly. 'He's dead.'

Paris, January 1830

NOTES

1. The Carraccis were three Italian Baroque artists from Bologna: Annibale (1560 – 1609), his brother Agostino (1557 – 1602) and their cousin Lodovico (1555 – 1619).

2. Napoleon Bonaparte (1769 – 1821) was born in Corsica. In 1799, he seized power in a coup d'état and became First Consul. Five years later he declared himself Emperor of France.

3. '*maquis*': from the Corsican Italian word *macchia*, meaning brushwood. The maquis was a highland of dense scrub, where outlaws would take refuge. It came to denote various guerrilla or resistance movements, most famously the French Resistance of the Second World War.

4. Antinoüs (110 – 130 AD), the lover of the Roman Emperor Hadrian, was deified by Hadrian after drowning in the Nile.

5. '*jocoso*': a comic character, a jester.

6. Pierre Paul Prudhon (1758 – 1823) was a French Neoclassical painter who painted Napoleon's wife Joséphine in 1805.

7. The Hundred Days was the period between Napoleon's return to Paris from exile in Elba and the restoration of the Bourbon dynasty under Louis XVIII. Soon afterwards, Napoleon was defeated at the Battle of Waterloo.

8. '*Eccola*': Italian for 'Here she is'.

9. On 15th July 1815, Napoleon surrendered to the captain of HMS *Bellerophon* and was kept on board as a prisoner for three weeks, until being transported to St Helena for life imprisonment.

10. Labédoyère: the first of Napoleon's soldiers to be arrested and tried for treason against the King, the young Colonel Labédoyère was brought to trial on 14th August 1815 and executed two days later.

11. Girodet: Anne-Louis Girodet de Triosson, 1767 – 1824, was a French Romantic painter who painted members of Napoleon's family.

12. Marshal Ney: Michel Ney, 1769 – 1815, was sentenced to death for treason by the Bourbons after siding with Napoleon during the 100 Days' War.

13. Salvator Rosa: 1615 – 73, Italian Baroque painter, poet and printmaker.

14. Marshal Feltre was Marshal of France in 1816, under Louis XVIII.

15. Abbé Vertot (1655 – 1735) was a French historian who uttered the phrase 'My siege is over' in response to an offer of additional data for his *History of the Knights Hospitallers* – indicating that he already had all the information he needed and did not need to add anything further.

16. Pierre Daru (1767 – 1829) was a French administrator and Secretary of War who was highly prized by Napoleon.

17. Antoine Drouot, 1774 – 1847, was one of Napoleon's generals.

18. Carnot: 1753 – 1823, Lazare Nicholas Marguerie, Comte Carnot, was a French politician and mathematician who served Napoleon and was exiled to Warsaw after the restoration of the Bourbon monarchy.

19. 'the disaster of Fontainebleau': After being defeated militarily by Russia and Britain, Napoleon abdicated, signing the Treaty of Fontainebleau on 11th April 1814.

20. Jean-Victor Schnetz (1787 – 1870) was a French academic painter.

21. 'Valide Sultan' was the title given to the mother of a Sultan in the Ottoman Empire.

Honoré de Balzac was born in Tours in 1799. His father was a state prosecutor in Paris, but was transferred to Tours during the French Revolution due to his political opinions. The family returned to Paris in 1814.

Balzac spent his early years in foster care, and did not excel at school. He went on to study at the Collège de Vendôme and the Sorbonne, before taking up a position at a law office. In 1819 his family was forced to move from Paris for financial reasons. They settled in the small town of Villeparisis whereupon Balzac announced that he wanted to be a writer and returned to Paris. His early works, however, went largely unnoticed. In order to increase his reputation in the literary world, Balzac entered the publishing and printing business, but this enterprise was not a success and left him with heavy debts, which were to dog him for the rest of his life.

Dispirited, Balzac moved to Brittany in search of new inspiration, and in 1829 *Les Chouans* appeared. This was a historical novel in the style of Sir Walter Scott and marked the beginning of his recognition as a writer. Between 1830 and 1832 he published six novelettes entitled *Scènes de la Vie Privée*.

In 1833 he had the idea of linking together his existing writings to form one extensive work encompassing the whole of society. This led to the remarkable *Comédie humaine* – a work of some ninety-one novels, with a cast of in excess of 2,000 characters, providing a comprehensive image of the life, habits and customs of the French bourgeoisie. Among the most celebrated works of the *Comédie humaine* are *La Peau de chagrin* (1831), *Les Illusions perdues* (1837–43), *La Rabouilleuse* (1840) and *La Cousine Bette* (1846). Balzac spent fourteen to sixteen hours a day writing in order to fulfil his ambitious plans.

During the later years of his life, Balzac befriended Eveline Hanska, a rich Polish lady, through a series of letters, and then, in 1848, he travelled to Poland to meet her. Despite his failing health, the two were married in 1850, although their marriage was to prove short-lived as Balzac died only three months later, on 18th August, in Paris.

Howard Curtis lives and works in London. He has translated many books from French and Italian, mostly fiction, including *The Way of the Kings* by André Malraux, *A Private Affair* by Beppe Fenoglio, and *The Turn* by Luigi Pirandello, all published by Hesperus Press. His translation of Edoardo Albinati's *Coming Back*, also published by Hesperus Press, won the 2004 John Florio Prize for Italian Translation.

SELECTED TITLES FROM HESPERUS PRESS

Author	Title	Foreword writer
Pietro Aretino	*The School of Whoredom*	Paul Bailey
Pietro Aretino	*The Secret Life of Nuns*	
Jane Austen	*Lesley Castle*	Zoë Heller
Jane Austen	*Love and Friendship*	Fay Weldon
Honoré de Balzac	*Colonel Chabert*	A.N. Wilson
Charles Baudelaire	*On Wine and Hashish*	Margaret Drabble
Giovanni Boccaccio	*Life of Dante*	A.N. Wilson
Charlotte Brontë	*The Spell*	
Emily Brontë	*Poems of Solitude*	Helen Dunmore
Mikhail Bulgakov	*Fatal Eggs*	Doris Lessing
Mikhail Bulgakov	*The Heart of a Dog*	A.S. Byatt
Giacomo Casanova	*The Duel*	Tim Parks
Miguel de Cervantes	*The Dialogue of the Dogs*	Ben Okri
Geoffrey Chaucer	*The Parliament of Birds*	
Anton Chekhov	*The Story of a Nobody*	Louis de Bernières
Anton Chekhov	*Three Years*	William Fiennes
Wilkie Collins	*The Frozen Deep*	
Joseph Conrad	*Heart of Darkness*	A.N. Wilson
Joseph Conrad	*The Return*	Colm Tóibín
Gabriele D'Annunzio	*The Book of the Virgins*	Tim Parks
Dante Alighieri	*The Divine Comedy: Inferno*	
Dante Alighieri	*New Life*	Louis de Bernières
Daniel Defoe	*The King of Pirates*	Peter Ackroyd
Marquis de Sade	*Incest*	Janet Street-Porter
Charles Dickens	*The Haunted House*	Peter Ackroyd
Charles Dickens	*A House to Let*	
Fyodor Dostoevsky	*The Double*	Jeremy Dyson
Fyodor Dostoevsky	*Poor People*	Charlotte Hobson
Alexandre Dumas	*One Thousand and One Ghosts*	

Francis Petrarch	*My Secret Book*	Germaine Greer
Luigi Pirandello	*Loveless Love*	
Edgar Allan Poe	*Eureka*	Sir Patrick Moore
Alexander Pope	*The Rape of the Lock* and *A Key to the Lock*	Peter Ackroyd
Antoine-François Prévost	*Manon Lescaut*	Germaine Greer
Marcel Proust	*Pleasures and Days*	A.N. Wilson
Alexander Pushkin	*Dubrovsky*	Patrick Neate
Alexander Pushkin	*Ruslan and Lyudmila*	Colm Tóibín
François Rabelais	*Pantagruel*	Paul Bailey
François Rabelais	*Gargantua*	Paul Bailey
Christina Rossetti	*Commonplace*	Andrew Motion
George Sand	*The Devil's Pool*	Victoria Glendinning
Jean-Paul Sartre	*The Wall*	Justin Cartwright
Friedrich von Schiller	*The Ghost-seer*	Martin Jarvis
Mary Shelley	*Transformation*	
Percy Bysshe Shelley	*Zastrozzi*	Germaine Greer
Stendhal	*Memoirs of an Egotist*	Doris Lessing
Robert Louis Stevenson	*Dr Jekyll and Mr Hyde*	Helen Dunmore
Theodor Storm	*The Lake of the Bees*	Alan Sillitoe
Leo Tolstoy	*The Death of Ivan Ilych*	
Leo Tolstoy	*Hadji Murat*	Colm Tóibín
Ivan Turgenev	*Faust*	Simon Callow
Mark Twain	*The Diary of Adam and Eve*	John Updike
Mark Twain	*Tom Sawyer, Detective*	
Oscar Wilde	*The Portrait of Mr W.H.*	Peter Ackroyd
Virginia Woolf	*Carlyle's House and Other Sketches*	Doris Lessing
Virginia Woolf	*Monday or Tuesday*	Scarlett Thomas
Emile Zola	*For a Night of Love*	A.N. Wilson